Copyright ©

All rights reserved. In accordance with the U.S.
Copyright Act of 1976.

ISBN 9781546326632

Acknowledgments

I would like to first thank God for giving me the mind to do what I have wanted to do for a long time, tell a story. There were times that I became discouraged because of the content, but I felt that people (mostly women), needed to know some things. I also want to thank my son, Dr. Jerome Anderson for always telling me I can do it, I love you to the moon and back son. My daughter-in-law Sheri, and those beautiful grandchildren of mine Cameron, Kaela, and Kailana, that are always loving on me; making me feel like the Queen of the jungle. To my siblings James Jr., Carol, Gwen(Pinky),Gloria, and Faye, who always tell me I think I'm the boss of them, thank you all so much for your support. And to my diva girls, Revelyn, MeMe, Courtney, Kathy Kakes, Marchelle Vernell, and Sharlette with an S, for telling me: "hurry up and put this book out there Phyl, women want to read about something that's real and relatable, but scared to share". Also I want to thank some of my male partners who told me to do that darn thing, SRV, GK, TD, TG and DR! I love you all for believing in me. To the late Mr. and Mrs. Jean/James Anderson who bought me into this world, they would be so proud of their baby girl; I love and miss you guys. To my cousin Shirley C, I could never forget how you stood in my corner since I was 12 years old, always encouraging me and was with me via email while I was going through my undergrad; thank you so much. To my St. Louis Public Schools family Sylvia Shead, who adopted me as her little sister and pushed me to become all I can be. Stephen Warmack, who believed in me and encouraged me to pursue all of my goals, Dr. Miranda Avant-Elliott who encourages me regularly to advocate for myself and see my self-worth as a leader, and Relana King and Wanda Cole for their support on the perfect design for my book cover.

Finally, I want to thank the folks who brought and read this book, booksellers and anybody else who supports me. This is a first for me and as I got to the finished line my son, Dr. Jay, Yaphett Elamin, and Bonita Cornute overwhelmed me with the advertisement and business part of this journey. I wasn't ready for that part, but thank you guys for opening my eyes. When I listen to people like Steve Harvey, Tyler Perry, Oprah Winfrey, Joel Osteen, and T. D. Jakes, I am so inspired and I decided that it was time for me to take the JUMP! The sequel will be coming soon........ .

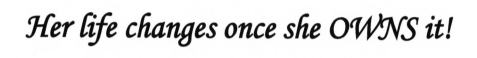

Her life changes once she OWNS it!

Chapter 1

I'm 25 years old and at a point in my life where my income was not sufficient to properly care for my son who was 6 years old at the time, drive the type of car I drove and live out on my own. So needless to say, Tyrone and I were forced to continue to live with my parents. I was working at PRA-TV, Channel 5, and was feeling the need for a career change. My brother and me discussed the possibilities of me becoming a police officer, which was the career he had chosen for himself. He advised me of the pay increase that I would receive and the great benefits and perks that came with the job. I applied for the job, got my acceptance letter, started the police academy in the spring, May of 1983 and became a real police officer September 8, 1983.

Keep in mind that I always wanted to be in control, the youngest of 5, and my need for more money and controlling any situation that I encountered, I felt this would be a great job. It is a statistical fact that the order of birth in families brings personal orders of priorities and again, being the youngest of 5, you'll see it had to be my way. This was the turning point of my life.

The class of 83 was in an assembly at the police academy where we were given the precinct in which we would be working in. I was sent to Precinct 12. I was okay with that because 12 was north and I knew nothing about the south side. A couple of my girls that I met and became cool within the police academy went south.

My first day on the job was on a Monday afternoon, on the (3-11pm) watch. Let us remember, I am a very statuette sister, 5'9," coffee brown completion, figure all together, hazel eyes, and long hair. As I was getting dressed for my first day on the job, I realized that my hair could not touch my collar; I looked in the mirror and said "I can see this shit ain't gonna work. They are messing with my swag". I finished dressing, put on my Michael Kor (sexy amber) perfume, looked at myself, and said, I'm getting ready to go kick some ass! I got into my White Mercedes Benz, turn on the radio and rode in listening to Frankie Beverly and Maze—Golden time of Day.

I parked my vehicle, said a prayer, got out of the car and walked into the police station. Old and young officers were around the station getting ready for roll call. I could hear some of the officer's saying damn, a sister looks good, and another responded the sharks are coming out and that sister is about to be bitten! I continued to walk down the hall and into the roll call room. The sergeant called the room to order and introduced all of the new officers. All of the new officers were given a training officer. That officer had five or more years on the force. They were to guide the new officers and they could literally determine someone's fate on the job.

I was assigned to a short female about 4'9" for a training officer. Wow! We looked like mutt and Jeff. I felt okay about that because after surfing the room and observing some very handsome bothers, I thought to myself, thank you Jesus, I can see me getting in trouble with some of these fine ass niggas! Most men think that when an attractive woman comes on the set, and they go after them, they think they're the ones doing the pursuing, like the brothers' that were talking under their breath about me "getting bit", not in my case. My state of mind is that of a man. All the time while I was in roll call, I was surfing the room and pinpointed who was going to become one of my victims.

Roll call was over! My training officer and I hit the streets and after going on several calls, I'm thinking to myself I think I have run into Victim number one! He was a 6'3', dark skinned brother, muscles all over the place, black natural curly hair (Ummm). He didn't come out of Precinct 12. He was working in a unit that I later found out was called

Mobile Reserve. I notice that every time I got a call, he was parked somewhere near watching and depending on the call he would get out his car. Finally I asked my training officer who was the guy in the car marked MR just watching us. She said "oh that's the Mobile Reserve Unit, they ride all over the city and depending on the area of the call they will come by just to offer assistance". I said oh ok" and all along thinking to myself, damn that nigga is fine! After we finished one of the calls, he finally got out of the car, walked over to us, and spoke. He knew my training officer and said, "What's up Shazell"? "Nothing much Ken;" "I got a prob with me, trying to teach her the ropes". "I know you are going to give it to her raw Zell, you know that's how you get down baby girl". Now mind you my training officer is 4'9," dreaded hairstyle, no shape, and smokes a cigar. Need I say anything else? He finally addresses me. "Hi …I said Pam Greer is my name," "he said hi Ms. Pam Greer I'm Kenneth Rhythm; is that Miss or Mrs.

Pam Greer"? "I said the first, and is that Mr. and Mrs. Kenneth Rhythm"? He paused, and said "the first and they call me Ken". I knew he was lying but needless to say I was on mission and little did he know he was about to become my first victim. We walked over to the side where we had more privacy. He looked me up and down and said, "Ms. Pam Greer, I hope you don't mind me saying this, but baby you are so fine". He then asked could we talk later. I told him yes and gave him the digits. He gave me is cell number, and that was fine by me. I noticed that after I got back in the car my training officer looked at me strange. "So what's up with Mr. Ken"? She looked at me with a tone of "as if you didn't know, without saying it". I said "well I'm waiting, what is going on with him"? She said "now you know he is married". I'm thinking, how in the hell am I supposed to know this man was married, Really! "Shazell how was I supposed to know that he is married"? I'm thinking to myself, why is she acting like she's pissed off that he's married. I thought he asked me for my number. We went on to our next call and there he was again. OMG! This time I saw him in action. The call was for a fight and when we got there Kenny had taken control. I had never seen anything like it. When he and his partner were through with those guys I bet they wished the police were never called. Kenny and his partner beat the breaks off those cats. All I could think of was I wonder what he's like in bed. Yeah I said it. And I'm going to find out!

Chapter 2

A couple of days went by and no call from Mr. Kenny Rhythm. I was not going to make the first call. Finally on the third day after meeting him, my phone rang. Ring, ring, ring…". Hello," "Hi" "may I speak to Pam"? "This is she". "Hey Pam did I catch you at a bad time"? "No, what's up"? "Are you busy this weekend, do you have to work"? "No I'm off this weekend and I don't have anything planned". "I'd like to take you out for dinner if that's okay with you". Now check this out, he knew I wasn't working because my training officer told me that he asked her what platoon/bracket we were on and she told him. So he knew my schedule; another game. I said "why Mr. Kenny Rhythm are you asking me out on a date"? "Why Miss Pam Greer, that is exactly what I'm doing". "I would be honored to go out to dinner with you". "What time will you be by to get me"? "How does 7 pm sound"? "That's good". "Okay I will see you Saturday at 7".

It's Saturday evening, around 3ish. I'm going through my closet trying to find the most seductive dress I have. It is a beautiful day in September and the breeze is coming through my bedroom window determining what I should wear. Got it! My LBD. Every woman has a LBD—Little Black Dress; like every woman should have a TM. Of course my LBD fits my bod and then I'll put on my sexy 3" sandals that will pronounce those calves I've been working on so hard. I laid out my accessories, and oh yeah that magic smell good (MK—Sexy Amber) that is going to have that nigga all over me. I went in my workout room, got on my TM for a quick 45-minute run, and then took a shower. Running makes me feel so powerful, the adrenalin rushes through me and I just feel like I can conquer the world. Especially, "Mr. Kenny Rhythm; better known as victim # 1".

It's about 6 o clock now and I'm playing 94. 4 oldies radio station and KIDD T is doing the damn thing. I mean he is playing Maze, Luther, and my all-time favorite, The Temptations. I'm penning up my hair, make-up all fresh, not too much, grooving with the beats and sipping on a glass of wine. I must say I look fabulous!

Well victim # 1 arrived a little early. My parents and my son were gone. Kenny rings the doorbell. I opened the door with a look so seductive that he couldn't even say hi. He just starred … "hello, how are you"? "Oh I'm sorry baby, how are you this evening"? "You look fabulous"! "Thank you, you look nice also". "Are you ready baby"? "Yes, let me lock up". We walked to his Triple black Cadillac, he opens the door for me and stood there until I was situated with my seat belt on, and then walked around and got in. He gazed over at me and said; "Pam you are so beautiful, too beautiful to be a police officer". "Why thank you Sir". We drove away listening to some jazz, which sounded real good. We went to a restaurant called Lombardo's. Lombardo's is an upscale restaurant in the central west end where you will find upscale people. In other words, a restaurant that you wouldn't see many of us in (see where I'm going with this)! So the night was young and Kenny was putting down his smooth game. We went round and round about my becoming a police officer. I really wanted to tell him enough of the small talk, why don't you really say what you want with me, but I didn't. I finally said "so what is a handsome young man like yourself doing single and a police officer"? "Well Pam I need to let you know something about my status". I'm thinking to myself, let the games begin. This is gone be good! "What part did you leave out Kenny"? "Well I am married, but we are not doing well at this time in our marriage; as a matter of fact, we are in two different bedrooms". "I have two small children and I really want to be in their lives; I want them to wake up with me in the house every day". I'm thinking to myself, and the look on my face must be saying this nigga is a damn fool if he thinks I believe that BS that he is putting down, but it's all good because all I want is a little fun with him and I'm moving on. You see I work out at the gym in the police academy. I run in the mornings when I'm on the afternoon watch and about 11:00 o'clock or so, a group of guys are there playing basketball. Man I am telling you it is on and popping. Niggas' out the why zoo from all precincts are there. It is so thick down there I don't know what to do with myself. So this crock of mess Kenny is talking is fine by me.

I finally chimed in and said "well Kenny I'm sorry to hear that about your marriage". "I'm single with a 7-year-old son. His father is absent in his life, but my family are truly a great help to me regarding him. And as far as me becoming a police officer, well it was a means to an end so to speak. I am dating, not serious nor am I looking to marry anytime soon, so no there is no one special in my life". "Thank you Lord, I don't know what I would do if you told me you were seeing someone Pam". "Why is that Kenny"? "Baby I really want to get to know you; with my circumstances being what they are, I just didn't know what or how you would feel about it". "That's cool Kenny, and I do appreciate you letting me make my own decision regarding if I want to continue to see you".

We left the restaurant and Kenny asked if we could go riding. I'm thinking to myself go riding, nigga as good as I'm looking you want to go riding, really. Needless to say I agreed. He started talking about his family again, trying to convince me that nothing sexually was going on between him and his wife. I could care less because I was going to hit that and be gone. We must have ridden around for about 2 hours before he finally said "Pam would you be my lady"? I smirked and said "Kenny I will go out with you, but baby I don't know you like that to make a commitment tonight; I mean it's only been one date". "Baby I know, but I am so sure about you". "Just give me a chance". I'm saying to myself, damn this is going to be easier than I thought. "Well Kenny like I said, I will go out with you but baby I can't make a commitment". "Okay Pam, I tell you what, just give me a chance to prove to you my sincerity. At this point all I could do was say okay to keep this nigga from beginning to sound like he was begging. "Ok Kenny, do your thang baby".

The night ended at about 12:30am. He walked me to the door, we said our good nights and I went in the house thinking, damn I don't know if I want to take him on, he sounds like he can turn into a fatal attraction. I could not wait to call "D". "What's up "D"?" "Hey Pam, what's going on girl"? "Girl I went out with victim #1 and I think he is going to be easy girl". "Why you say that"? "Girl this motherfucker asked me to be his lady"! "Girl you lying"! "No "D," I thought to myself…. "are you serious"? "I could not believe he wanted me to commit to him on the first date". "So what did you tell him Pam"? "I told him lets continue to go out

14

and see where we land". "OMG! That was an easy one Pam". "D" I don't think I want to do him". "Oh girl you always put your feelings in the way". "No, it's not that my feelings are in the way, he seems like he is very genuine". "Pam, are you serious, if he was genuine he would be with his wife". "Pam when we started this project we said we didn't want Mr. Right or Mr. Perfect"! "We are conductors of our train's and pilots of our planes no matter which they decide to ride"! "We are not doing the Steve Harvey "90" rule". "You are going to have to make up your mind baby girl". "This is a game that when played you are going to have to set your feelings to the side are they will be walked on". "This job is not the place to find your knight in shining amour"! "Don't even try it"! "We are not getting ready to feed these motherfuckers' egos; this is getting ready to be about us"!

Chapter 3

Dirty "D"

It's Monday morning and I'm headed down to the gym to go running. Of course I have on the cutest running clothes and hair pinned up, and yes you said it, face made up! I start running at around 10 or so. I had to get my run in before I became distracted. After the sermon Pastor "D" preached last night, needless to say it was about to be on. It is 11:40 am, and like clockwork the guys from every precinct were engaged in a basketball game. Some of them were in great shape and some looked okay, nothing to write home about. The one that really stood out to me was one that I peeped in roll call out at precinct 12. His name was Earl Brannon. He was about 6'2," nice build, very handsome brother, but very arrogant. He stood out to me because he was the type that I relish in breaking down like a shot gun. He talks big SHIT! I finished working out and as I was headed out Mr. Earl Brannon happened to be heading out the door as well. "What's up Ms. Pam"? "Hey, how are you doing"? "I'm sorry, what's your name again, I forgot"? "Earl" "Hey Earl, how you doing today"? (Earl gave me a look as if to say, I know you didn't forget my name)! "Looks like you got it in today". "Yeah I had to let them niggas know I still got game". I'm saying to myself, yeah right, you got game alright, about to fall out, gasping for air. "Yeah, I saw you getting it in Earl". "So Pam what's up with you for the rest of the day"? "Nothing much, I'm about to go home and rest up for work this evening". "Me too, you want to pick up some lunch first"? "Yeah, that sounds good; I can use a salad right about now". "Cool, let me get your number and address and I'll call you when I finish cleaning up". "Okay". I gave victim # 2 the digits and my address. About an hour later he called and said he was on his way. I got ready, and again it's that fall weather so we got a little Indian summer going on. It's about 78 degrees out and a light breeze. I put on a pair of my apple bottom jeans, some 3" sandals and a cute top. I let my hair down and oh yeah, I put on some that killer MK (Sexy Amber) perfume that I knew was going to send that nigga through the roof. We headed down to the central west end and Earl said how does Culpepper's sound? I told him that was real cool. I knew I could get a salad that would keep me on full until it was time for me to eat dinner at work. As I said earlier, Earl was so damn arrogant; he made you sick to the stomach. We're trying to find a parking space for his convertible triple black Corvette that I think he believes is his woman for real. He was sporting some Tommy jeans, a sweater that was fitting his bod, and some loafers. I ain't gonna lie; the nigga was smellin good and looked the part. If he wasn't so damn arrogant, I think I would see him differently. Any whoo, we finally parked, went inside the restaurant, got seated and ordered our food. Once the waitress took our orders we small talked about our careers. Now the one thing I did like about Earl was that he didn't have any children and was single, or should I say, not committed. No momma drama! The other cool thing was that he just happened to live around the corner from my mom and dad. That meant I wasn't going to have to go very far to score. We finished lunch, parted and said we would see each other in a few. When I got to work and walked into the roll call room, I noticed that the other guys were kind of stand offish. Not like they were when I first came there. I'm thinking I know this nigga didn't label me as marked because it was one of those types of looks. I knew one of the guys standing by the copier, his name was Rue. Rue and I went way back. His wife and I went to high school together. I waited until after roll call and for Earl to leave out of the precinct. I cornered Rue and asked him did Earl say anything about us going out to lunch. He said "Pam, let me say this to you baby girl, when new meat come into the precinct, it gets marked real quick". "Yeah Earl put the word out". "I said oh okay". I'm thinking now, I'm going to get this trick!

My shift is over and I'm pissed the F***K off! I called my girl "D," birth name Diana Crenshaw, better known as Dirty D. Diana and I went through the police academy together. Dirty D was no joke in the streets. Me and a couple of other girls gave that name to Diana in the police academy because she schemed her way through so smooth. Diana was about 6'0," bi-racial, beautiful long hair, grey eyes, and a shape to die for. Diana didn't have any children and that was good because she was something else. She was the type that did and said what others wanted to do and say, but didn't. "What's up 'D', hey girl". "How is it going"? "Girl 'D', I am pissed". "What's up, I thought you had all of your victims in order over there". "I'm having a ball over in precinct 16. "Girl I'm getting ready to show these brothers' how the game is really played". "You know how we fought in high school over the football boys; that's how I'm going to have them". "'D' this victim # 2 got me confused girl". "We had lunch one time and he has a mark over me like I'm his woman". "No he don't girl". "Yes"! "You know it is on now"! "I'm getting ready to show him how this shit works". "You know Pam, I told you, you spend too much time with these niggas' which creates drama". "You know the game, hit it and keep moving". "Stop acting brand new about this, you get too caught up". "Now here is what you do to that MF": "Put his ass on some ice". "What do you mean"? "Never avail yourself to him and go back and work on victim #1". "Play around with V#1 for a while and then catch back up with that bastard".

I took Dirty 'D's advice and called Kenny. Needless to say Kenny was very excited to hear from me. "Hi Kenny"! "Hey Pam, how are you baby"? "I'm good; I've been a little busy with my son back in school along with his afterschool activities". "You know the routine". "Yeah, been there, done that". "Pam I really wish you would consider what we talked about the last time we were together". For one I couldn't believe Kenny was still on having a serious relationship, for two, I couldn't believe that he couldn't see where I was coming from. "Kenny let's just go out baby and let nature take its course". "I guess I'll have to be good with that". "I don't want you to think I'm a stalker". "So do you have anything going on this weekend"? "Not too much, my girl 'D' and I were going to hook up". "Are you talking about Diana Crenshaw"? "Yeah; why"?

"Pam, are you all close because word is out that she is something else". Damn, he's a gossiper! "That sounds about right and why the word is out; they better put the word out that she is no joke"! We both laughed. "Pam I wanted to see if you wanted to do dinner and a movie". "That sounds good Kenny, I will call you back later to confirm, and I need to let 'D' know I'm changing course on her". "She won't mind". "Ok, I look forward to hearing from you baby". Ring, Ring, Ring, I looked at my phone and was Earl's ass! I let the call go to voice mail and continued on. I texted "D" and told her I was going to kick it with Kenny. She was cool with it; whenever we were going to change course for a brother, it was always cool. I called Kenny back and told him we were on, but I wasn't as excited as I was when I first met him. He kind of seems unbalanced or maybe unsure of himself. His persona led one to believe that women were kicking his door down if you know what I mean.

Kenny and I hooked up and headed to the movies. As he walked around and let me in he reached over and kissed me. OMG! It was a bummer. All of this fine ass man and he can't kiss! I couldn't believe it. At this point I didn't want to try anything else. All I could think of was how am I going to end this night. If you couldn't kiss, that was a deal breaker for me. I know what I can say to end the night---I'll get some popcorn and then I'll tell him that the popcorn didn't agree with my stomach so he can take me home. I was so disappointed. He went for it and I could not wait to tell "D".

Ring…"What's up "D"? "Hey girl, I know your date is not over yet". "Girl this nigga was a bummer"! "Why"? "D" he couldn't kiss". "You know how I feel about kissing"! "Girl you couldn't get pass that"? "No, "D" I couldn't; I faked stomach ache". "Pam you could have gotten pass that and seen what the rest was like". "Not tonight, maybe another time". "You might as well; you know he is going to blow your phone up". "If you are not going to deal with him you need to drop him". "Yeah, I know". "Girl he is so fine; I would have thought he could at least kiss". "I was not trying to teach any of my victim's girl"; "I just want to hit it and keep going". "I don't know Pam; I think I could get past the kissing and see what was up with a brother".

"Damn girl you talked me into it". "I guess I'll give him a call and apologize for getting sick". "Call him now Pam, you know he is still up or should I say, if he is not sleeping in the same bed with his wife he should be able to answer the phone". "Yeah you got a point". "Let me call him, I'll hit you back". That damn "D" could remember everything you tell her about somebody, but she was right; let me see what is going on with Mr. Kenny. I think I will text him and see if he texts me back or calls me. Hey Kenny, just letting you know I had a great night and my tummy is feeling a lot better. I will call you tomorrow. Time will tell what he is made of. Uh oh…do I hear a ring coming through from Mr. Kenny? Well I do believe it is Mr. Kenny. "Hi baby". "Hey how do you feel"? "I'm better Kenny, thanks for asking". "I am so sorry our night had to end so early". "That's okay baby, another time". "I know, but I was looking forward to being with you tonight". "Don't worry Pam; another time will present itself". "Kenny are you free the rest of the weekend". "Yeah baby, what do you have in mind"? "Let's get a suite at the Ramada". "I already have one booked for the weekend baby". "What"! "Yes, I wanted to surprise you after the movies, but you got ill". "Where do you have it booked"? "I booked three nights/four days at the Chase". OMG! I was so glad I wasn't in his face so that he could not see my expression. "I tell you what, I'll pack me a bag and why don't you come over and get me". "I thought you would never ask; I'm on my way baby". "Okay". I hurried up, called "D" back, and told her what was up. "I told you girl, you betta go get what you went for"! "You are so funny "D". "I'm just saying, you about to put him down because he can't kiss, really"? "You betta teach him what you want him to do to you"! How about that! "Okay crazy woman, I will call you when I get back home"! "No"! "You sneak and text me throughout the weekend and let me know what that nigga is bringing to the table". "Girl okay, I'll talk to you later".

Since it was so late I told Kenny to text me when he was out front. I must admit I was excited to see what the weekend would turn out to be. I got my text and told my mom I was out for the weekend doing a girls thing. Yeah I know I'm grown, but it's something about telling your mom you are getting ready to go spend the weekend with a man, really! Well I wasn't about to tell old Jean that I was getting ready to make a co-worker a victim. There Kenny was standing outside of his car waiting to let me in; looking fine as ever. He kissed me on my cheek and said "baby I'm glad you called me". I smirked and said "I am to, and I'm so sorry I ended the movie like I did". "Pam that's no problem sweetheart, because if you allow me; we are going to make a movie". "Oh you are so cute Mr. Kenny". "I will be the director of this movie". "That is exactly what I want you to do, direct me baby"!

Well as the night went on I was indeed the director of this ship. I directed Mr. Kenny everywhere I wanted him to go. OMG! I thought he couldn't kiss, but something happened between time he kissed me earlier and now. Man! This brother not only could kiss but he knew how to work everything God gave him.

Chapter 4

The shift at work had changed and we're on days' now. It's our platoon's last day before going on a five day off cycle and it seems that the guys were feeling good this morning. Earl walked over to me after roll call and said, "what's up Pam, I tried calling you, but didn't get an answer, nor a call back". "Really, that meant I was busy Earl". "What's up"? "What's up"? "Is that how it is"? "What are you talking about Earl"? "You called, I didn't answer, and we see each other now, what's up"? "I was trying to see you this weekend". "I got plans for the weekend Earl". "Oh okay". Earl walked away with a bit of an attitude. I'm saying to myself, brother when I see you again it will be on my terms and not yours. As the day went on Earl was coming by my calls. After completing one of the calls I walked over and asked was he just looking out, or did he have something to say me.

"I'd like to talk to you if you don't mind". I looked over across the street at my training officer and she didn't have a happy look on her face. "what's on your mind". "Damn baby don't you think you could have called me back or something"? "Hey look Earl, we discussed that this morning and I'm not one of those people who continue to talk about the same thing over and over". "I say what I have to say and I move on". "So is there anything else you want, because my training officer looks a little pissed" and I need to go and see what's up with this bitch"! "Zell over there trippin with you"? "Yeah, this bitch is on some BS". "Every time I start talking with one of the guys, her attitude changes". "Come on now Pam, you don't know what's up"? "What do you mean I know what's up"? "Zell is gay baby". "No shit"? "Yeah"! "Well I'll be damn, so that's why she made that comment". "What comment baby"? "Let me get back over here Earl, I'll talk with you later". I went back over to the car and said hey I'm ready, sorry if

I took too long. She didn't say anything. We continued on our day and at the end of the night before our shift were over, our Lt. called me in. I walked into his office; Lieutenant Levi Brown was his name. "Good afternoon Ms. Greer". "Have a seat, thank you sir, good afternoon". "How is it going"? "I think it's going fine sir, so far I have no complaints".

Let me tell you a little bit about Lt. Levi Brown. Lt. Brown was known for being savvy with everything and everyone. He was called "Lightning" throughout the police department. Mr. Lightning was Tall, dark, and handsome as hell. One would find it very difficult to talk to him; the brother had some serious swag going on. He smelled good and one would say he had a superman body build. That made him stand out even more in his uniform. To put it simple, he was just plain old fine and known for doing what the hell he wanted to do. Well respected, or so I thought. "Officer Greer, let me tell you why I called you in, your training officer, Shazell, said you were not doing so well". "Her evaluation is saying that you don't listen very well and on this job that is a very important attribute". "I personally think that you can be taught how to do this job and we have spent too much money for your training to drop you from the roll". "When you come back from your 5 days off, I want you to come in prepared to ride with me, you won't need a vest or anything because we are going to ride and talk for a while". (Remember the swag I told you about). "Then I will decide who I am going to put you with". "Just go home and relax, everything is going to be okay". I thanked him and said okay sir, I will see you in five and I walked out thinking what did this bitch say about me?

I got into my car and cried out to God. I could not believe that this bitch would fuck with my lively hood and no doubt because I'm strictly dickly! And she's a sister, really! Ring, Ring… "What's up 'D'". "How you doing Pam"? "Call to let you know that they just dropped one of my P's". "I can ride by myself now". "Hey! That's great 'D'". "What's wrong with you"? "You don't sound good". "'D' girl, my training officer gave me a poor evaluation". "What"? "Yeah girl, and the Lt. wants me to come in when we come off of rec and ride with him for a while so that we can talk". "Girl you are lying"? "Nope"! "You know what's up Pam, the bitch is mad because all the niggas are on you". "Yeah, that's what Earl said". "Earl"? If that bastard knew what was up with her, how come he didn't warn you so that you could have played your cards a little different"? "Yeah I know". "Girl don't tell me anything else about Earl"! "I guess you know he doesn't have your best interest at heart". "Yeah 'D' I know". "'D' I can't believe this is happening". "I worked so hard in the academy and I listened to every word this bitch said to me and now all of sudden I'm not up to par". "Pam, I feel you girl". "But chill out". "Are you on your way home"? "Yeah, I'm pulling in now". "I'm on my way, we are going to figure this shit out". "Okay 'D', see you in a bit". I'm thinking to myself, what does Dirty 'D' have up her sleeves now. (Text coming through) "I'm here, come open the door". "What's up Ms. 'D', congrats girl on your dropping one of your Ps". "Thanks"! "I got us some wine girl; we are off for five, break out the glasses and let's do the damn thing". "Okay". I could tell by the look on 'D's face that this was going to be a long night, perhaps an all-nighter. At this point I didn't have nothing to lose. "By the way 'D' I mentioned to Kenny that I was calling you to let you know I had changed my plans and he said your name was all over the place". "Girl fuck Kenny, I'll rap to you later about that, let's get our plan ready for when you go back to work". 'D' started asking me questions about what went on with my training officer and started writing things down. She was so deep with it you would have thought she was a defense attorney. Hours had gone by and finally 'D' said okay Pam this is what you are going to say. I read what 'D' wrote and said "damn girl you are good". "Yo ass should have gone to law school instead of the police academy". We laughed, 'D' left and I went to bed.

Chapter 5

It was our first day back at work and I had rehearsed what 'D' and I discussed like it was a play. I wasn't feeling my best, but I was looking and smelling good. After roll call the sergeant told me to report to Lt. Brown's office. All the guys had a smirk on their faces like oh boy, 'Lightning is getting ready to tear into her ass. Another one spoke saying, in more ways than one. Needless to say I didn't trip off of what they were saying, I was wondering where that bitch was that put me in this situation. I surfed the room and didn't see Shazell. I'm thinking, where she could be today. Roll call was over and Earl walked up and asked what I thought my meeting with Lt. Brown was about. I played it off as if I didn't know. I told him that I was not sure and that I would talk to him later. I could not believe that son of a bitch. Word was out what Zell did. Why would he come to me and act like he didn't know? It's all good, because I was gunning after his ass very shortly.

I went to the Lt.'s office and he beckoned for me to come in and have a seat until he finished his phone call. Let us not forget how good this man looks and smells. Lt. Brown got off the phone and greeted me. He started adjusting his holster for his gun and said let's ride. Lt. Brown started asking me questions about my decision on becoming a police officer? I told him about my brother talking to me about a career change, who he knew, and he nodded his head as if to say, I hear you. He then started asking me things about my personal life which caused me to get a little uncomfortable, but I didn't let on. 'D' had me ready for any and all types of sceneries'. I was thinking to myself, where is he going with this line of questioning. Needless to say it was on now. After three hours of personal talk, I knew when I got out of his vehicle, I had no worries.

Lt. Brown let me go home early and told me not to worry about anything. He advised me that when I came to work tomorrow I would have a new training officer. I asked him did I have to do another 90 days; he paused, looked at me seductively and said, no, you don't.

When the guys saw that I had gone home early, they all wondered what had gone on. My phone was blowing up and I allowed all the calls go to my voice mail. I had one thing on my mind. How was I going to handle this situation with Lt. Levi Brown? I don't know why I was having a hard time figuring this out with him being married and all, but he was so fine and I knew with all the power he possessed, he was not going for me dealing with him and other guys in the precinct. So there goes the projects that me and "D" had planned. I'm also thinking about how I'm going to end this fatal attraction affair with Kenny, and how I just want to hit and miss on Earl's ass. Kenny I kind of felt sorry for because he was genuine. I believed he was in a messed up situation and really cared about me. Kenny would give me money and gifts on a regular basis. Earl on the other hand was out to get what he could and wanted to be able to tell the guys he scored. I was determined to put him on his ass! *(Pam's Pearl!)*

My phone was ringing and I could see that it was Kenny. I answered and we talked about my situation for a minute. I told him what the Lt. said he would do and Kenny got quiet. I ask him what was wrong and he advised me that I needed to be careful with that Lt. I asked him what he meant, all along knowing what was up. "Lt. Brown is something else and if I know him, Pam, trust and believe he has something else on his mind besides helping you". At this point in my life I didn't care about the warnings, I liked me some Lt. Brown. I decided that I would be honest with Kenny. "Kenny I can't see you anymore"! "Why Pam"? "I need to focus on raising my son". "Ok baby, I understand". After talking to Kenny, I my next move was to hit that Earl and move on. I was not going to let him off that easy. I called Earl later that evening and asked him if he wanted to go out for some dinner. I knew he would agree and we met at 7:30 at his house. I'm thinking to myself tonight is the night that I make him a victim. I will be gentle, but it's going down.

I called 'D'. "What's up chick"? "Wow, don't you sound happy today Ms. Pammy"! "Give me the 411"! "Girl I rode with Lt. Brown for 3 hours today". 'D' girl I wanted to ask him to pull over or go to a hotel". Girl he is so fine and got swag that won't quit. "Hold up Pam, I know you not giving up the plan for taking these tricks to the bank"? 'D' I like him". "Pam please tell me it ain't so"! "You've been bitten girl"! "Fuck you 'D'! "This man has power and I want some of it". "Pam girl he's married"! "Check my voice for a sound of concern"! "I'm not the first and I'm not going to be the last". "Pam you are getting off into some shit you can't control girl". "So what about Kenny and Earl"? "I broke if off with Kenny, but Earl, girl that punk was a waste of time". "I should have known because of all the talking he did. "However, the inquisitiveness is over for him". "So I guess you are going to go one on one with the Lt."? 'D' I don't think he would have any other way; especially with the guys in the precinct". "You know how men talk once they think they have scored". "Pam it sounds like you have made up your mind, but I think you need to give this some serious thought". "You know what 'D', I never say anything to you when you get out there and make bad choices". "I support you even if they are what I believe are bad decisions". "Why you can't support me on this one". "Pam I just see disaster coming out of this". "Why Lt. Brown, he's married"! "I guess for the same reason you chose Shaun". "Oh so we on some tit for tat bullshit"? 'D' you know Shaun came with at least ten different families, but did I say don't mess with him". "No"! "All I told you was that you got some shit on your hands, but I got faith in you, I know you can handle it". "My being with Shaun is totally different Pam". "No it's not 'D'; it is the same for women, broken is broken". "If he has that many families, he is no doubt a broken man". "He has to find himself first before he finds his mate or he will continue to damage any woman he comes in contact with which is apparently what he's doing and my dear you are next".

"And also let me say this 'D', I know what I'm doing is saying something about my character and probably even how I feel on the inside as well, but right now girl this is where I'm at, broken". "I don't want to deal with myself if you know what I mean". "But one thing about it 'D', I own my issues". *(Pam's Pearl!)* "Yeah Pam I hear you, I guess you are making a point". "I know I could do better, but it is something about Shaun that I like". "No 'D', you don't want to deal with your stuff either". "Damn Pam, that's deep". "We are pretty women, with nice careers, able to take care of ourselves, you got your Master's degree, but yet we settle for this bullshit". "Girl 'D' we could talk all night about this and one day this shit is going in my best seller book". "Yeah Pam, you're right girl, but I'm not giving up, in the midst of all the challenges I may encounter I am going to overcome these obstacles"! "Girl my phone is ringing; I'll be damned, it's Lt. Brown! "Girl I'm not ready to talk to him, he is going to voice mail".

Chapter 6
Levi Brown

It is late fall and somewhat of a breezy night. I am back on the 3-11pm watch and after making relief on the last day going into rec, Lt. Brown called me in his office. "Pam have seat baby. I don't know what's going on with you, but Officer Haley said he was having problems with you". "I tried to call you last night and got your voice mail and I didn't want to leave a message regarding the job on your voice mail". "Are you serious Lt. Brown"? "Yes baby I am so serious". "OMG"! "Lt. Brown, I have to defend myself sir". "This man is always trying to talk to me about things that are not pertaining to the job and I have told him I am not interested in him in that way". "I told him I just want to learn the job, but he is very persistent". "Sir this is just not fair". "Pam I believe you and I know what I'm going to do". "Are you busy tonight"? "No sir, at this point I need to go home and do some soul searching". "Do you mind meeting me for a drink at Carmines located inside of the Chase Park Plaza in the central west end"? "Sure". "I'm done so I'll head there now". "Ok, see you in a minute".

I arrived at the restaurant and Lt. Brown came up shortly after. He came to my car and we walked in and got seated. "Lt. Brown I don't know what to say about all of this". "Sir I know I can do this job". "Pam I know that you can to baby". "This is my game plan: I'm going to have you transferred over to Precinct 11". "I know everyone over there". "I have the perfect training officer for you". "He is well equipped to get you through this. Thank you so much. I don't know where I would be if you hadn't stepped in the way that you did. It's all good Pam; I don't want to see anyone that's trying to support their family out of a job, especially regarding a situation like this. I know your brother very well and I believe you are a good person that just so happen to need a break right now. I will set it up where you will do a month with him and then they will drop one of your P's baby. Thank you so much sir. Pam don't think about this job anymore. So tell me what's a beautiful young lady like you doing in this field of work? Well Lt. to make a long story short, it was more like a means to an end, but I'm wondering if I made the right decision now. I can't believe some of these people. It makes me wonder how in the hell can they go out and protect and serve when their own lives are so broken. I here you baby. Pam how does your man feel about you being a police officer? I don't have anyone special in my life with the exception of my 7-year-old son. Really! Yes, I broke up with someone right before I started the police academy. "So Lt., enough about me, what about you"? "Wife"? "Girlfriend"? "Well Pam, I'm married, but separated. What's up with that? We stopped getting along, everything started to become anti, I couldn't do anything right in her eyes and eventually I started looking at her the same way. Now we are looking into divorcing. Wow! So Lt. how do you feel about that; that's a big step? How many years were you all together? I'm sorry, one question at a time. Yeah baby it took its toll on me because we were together 15 years and that's a long time. But I have accepted it and adjusted to living life without her and I'm ready to move on.

Pam now that we've gotten our personal innuendo's out of the way I need you to know that I'm interested in you. Really! Yeah really! Well Lt. Brown, I'm interested in you too, but we have to do something about your name. What do you mean? I need a name for you. Oh really, is that so? Yep, and I think I know what it is. What? LB. Ha, ha! LB huh? Yep, you like it? Only coming from you baby. Ok LB it is. Lol! We ended the night at about 1:30 in the morning. He gave me his cell and private number to his office, a peck on the cheek and told me he would talk to me in the morning. We parted and I felt so good. I could not wait to call 'D' when I drove away. Ring? Who could this be this late? I looked down at my phone and it was Earl calling. Of course it is going to voice mail. I called 'D' and got her voice mail. I didn't bother to leave a message because neither of us ever listens to messages anyway. I got home and immediately checked in on Tyrone. I thought I heard my phone ringing and it was. To my surprise it was Lt. Brown, my bad, LB. Hey LB, what's up, did you forget something? I sure did, I was making sure you got home, but I forgot to get a hug! Oh really. Yes, really. But there will be next time. Next time when? What's on your agenda for tomorrow? I just cleared my agenda LB, you're funny Pam. You want to do dinner and a movie tomorrow? That sounds good. How does 6:00 o'clock sound? That's cool. Okay I'll see you then. Good night baby, good night LB.

Chapter 7

I can't remember sleeping so well! I was glad I was still on rec because the first thing on my agenda was to go look for me and Tyrone a place to stay. I had a couple of places lined up. The first place I saw was a huge house on Dryden. It looked like a one family house from the outside, but once you went inside there were steps that led to the second floor apartment. It had two bedrooms, living room, kitchen, and a bathroom to die for. The tub was so long; I had never seen a bathtub so long that when I sat in it I had at least four more inches to wiggle the water around. The bathroom was as big as Tyrone's room. The rent was up my alley and the Landlords appeared to be amazing. They had the downstairs and advised me that I could even use their washing area and the place was mine if I wanted it. I was on cloud nine. I didn't even have furniture. I went to the VV and got Tyrone a box spring and mattress and my mom let me bring one of her beds from her guest room. I don't know who was the happiest, me or mom. I told the land lord what I did for a living and they were happy as to peas in a pot. Their names were Mr. and Mrs. Brooks. Mrs. Brooks told me I could give her first and last month's rent and move in anytime I wanted. Well needless to say, living with my parents, and making the kind of money I was making, I moved right in. I called LB and told him the good news, he sounded very happy of course. He even asked me what he could do for me. I told him I needed a few odds and INS and he said he would be over when he got off work. I gave him the address and he said he would see me soon.

With what I had at my parents' house, I was moved in two hours. Like clockwork, LB came over when his shift ended. He looked the place over, gave his approval, gave me one thousand dollars, and told me to get what I needed and if I needed anything else just let him know. I looked at him and said really, thank you. He said no problem baby; I want you and Tyrone comfortable. I had the biggest smile on my face and hugged him tightly. OMG! I finally felt the muscles. His body felt so good next to mine and he smelled so good. If I didn't know any better, I think I could fall in love with this man. He asked me were we still on for tonight and if so call him when I got freed up and left.

I went back to a second hand shop that I saw when I was riding around while at work. They had everything you could use in a house. I got my chest and dresser's, lamps, kitchen supplies, the works. I went to Famous and Barr and picked up me some linen. I was so excited and could not wait to pick Tyrone up from my parent's house to show him his new room.

Tyrone had no idea we were moving. When I walked in the house, I told him to hurry up and finish eating because I had a big surprise for him. He had a happy face on and got finished eating.

We drove over to our new place and got out of the car. Tyrone kept saying momma where are we going. When he saw me put the key in the door, he yelled we moved momma; I got a new room! Yes, you do son! Momma I love it! Can we stay now? Yes, we can. We have to go and let grandma and grandpa know that we are spending the night at our new place and say goodbye. Okay momma, but can we hurry, I want to play in my new room. Boy please, don't act as if you are in a hurry to leave or you might hurt grandpa's feelings. Okay momma. I'm going to give them a big hug and tell them I am going to spend the night with them all the time. Good. But before we go baby lets go down stairs and meet the landlord. Who is that momma? Those are the people that we pay the rent to and they live downstairs as well. Hi Mr. and Mrs. Brooks. This is my son Tyrone. Hi Tyrone, how are you son? Hey there boy, how you doing? Are you going to help me cut the grass? Tyrone smiled and said yes Sir; I help my grandpa in his yard all the time. Mr.

and Mrs. Brooks smiled and told Tyrone they were glad to have him there.

I could see them all bonding and the Brook's being a second set of grandparents to Tyrone. Tyrone and I went back over to my parent's house and said our goodbyes for the evening. I don't know what the big deal was because my dad always picked Tyrone up from school, made sure he did his homework, and fed him dinner. I think Tyrone was excited that he had his own room to go to now. At my parents' house we shared a room. But trust and believe I was just as excited as he was. It got so late I decided to leave LB a text and told him to stop by in the morning.

Chapter 8

It's Saturday morning and I'm cooking for the first time in my new kitchen! I am excited and I cannot wait to wake up Tyrone. I'm wondering what it's going to be like when I introduce Tyrone to LB! "Good morning momma". Hi baby, you ready for breakfast? "Yes ma'am! I want pancakes and bacon". Oh really now. "Yes really now". Pancakes and Bacon coming up young man! Tyrone and I sat down to eat breakfast. I asked him what he thought about mommy having a boyfriend. "I guess it's okay. Who is it momma"? Well you don't know him but I am very fond of him and he is a cop like me. "I guess that will be alright". "Why thank you sir". Tyrone and I were just about done eating and there was a knock on the door. I went to answer the door and it was LB. I was so glad to see him and excited about him meeting Tyrone. I greeted him wearing my boy shorts and a big T-shirt. He came in the kitchen where Tyrone was and I introduced the two. They seem to have clicked pretty well. "Hey Mr. LB you want to see my room". "Sure Tyrone, but please, just call me LB". "Okay, well come and see my room LB". They went into his room and Tyrone took him through all of his transformers and named every truck in his room. By this time, my dad called and told me to have Tyrone ready so they can go cut grass. I went to Ty's door and told him to get ready because Pop's was on his way to get him.

Ty left and finally I was alone with LB. I was so excited to be alone with LB in a private setting, that I did not know what to do with myself. I tried to ignore the fact that he looked and smelled so good. "Come on LB and let me show you around". I took him by his hand and we went into my bedroom. I looked him in his eyes and said, "this is the queen's room"! He smiled, embraced me and started kissing me. His touch was so soft and I could feel myself getting wet and him getting a woody. I was saying to myself, OMG, it is about to go down this morning, but to my surprise he asked to see the rest of the house. I'm thinking to myself, look around, nigga as hot as I am, we don't need to look any further. I took him around the place and then we went back to my bedroom and began to talk. "Pam you know I am much known around the department and people have been asking me why I took such an interest in helping you when I don't know you". "Okay and you said"? "Well I told them that first of all, I help whom I want to help, and you were not the first person I have ever helped". "What is the big deal"? "Well needless to say everybody thinks they know me and they see that you are gorgeous, so they think I want to date you". "Well you do don't you"? "Yes, I do Ms. Pam, but I just wanted you to know that there are going to be some people trying to get in our business". "So you say that to say what"? "That what we do is our business". "So in other words LB, you want me to be your secret"? "No baby, nothing like that". "I'm not trying to hide you, but I'm just saying our business is our business". "Okay, I get it; don't give the rumor mill anything to go on". "That's what I'm getting at baby; I wouldn't dare hide someone and beautiful as you are". At this point LB was putting it on heavy, and I was buying it. I told LB enough of the shoptalk, let's get comfortable and watch an afternoon movie or some sports. "I thought you would never ask". "College basketball sounds good right about now". "Are you hungry baby"? "I'll take whatever you got ready; you don't have to go out of the way". I fixed him a hoagie sandwich, grabbed some chips and a bottle of water. "Thanks baby, this looks good". "Wow"! "It is good"! LB ate his sandwich and watched the basketball game. When he got done eating, he looked at me in a seductive tone and said come here, I need my afternoon dessert now. LB started kissing me all over and my body started trembling uncontrollably. There was no stopping at this point. After stopping at Pam's Pearl, he looked up at me and said may I baby. I'm thinking to myself, nigga, you betta. I just nodded my head as best I could in a yes motion. That afternoon was the genesis of my saga with Lt. Levi Brown.

Chapter 9

LB left about fivish and I was on cloud nine. I called my parent's house to see if Tyrone was coming home and my dad said he was staying so that he could go to church with them in the morning. That was fine by me. I couldn't wait to hook up with "D". "What's up "D"? "I can't call it, what's up with you"? "Girl I hooked up with LB"! "OMG"! "Girl it was just as I imagined". "I'm on my way over Pam, I want to hear every detail". "Ok, see you in a bit". I started straightening up and unpacking the few things that my mom gave me. The place was immaculate. "D" rang the doorbell and when she got upstairs, she was amazed. "Pam this is so pretty". "Girl how does Tyrone like it"? "He loves it"! "D" Tyrone met LB". "Girl how did that go"? "Hold up Pam, get me something to snack on, I know this is gonna be good". "Girl you are crazy". "You want me to put you a sandwich together and some chips"? "That's cool". "Okay, he started off talking about the job and what his co-workers were saying about his interest in me". "I listened to what he had to say and summed it up as "are you trying to make me your little secret"? "Of course he said no, but just wanted me to know that the buzz was out there and to be ready for it". "I told him okay and enough of the small talk lets watch a movie or some sports". "He said great idea". "I fixed the famous Pam's hoagie sandwich, which I knew he would like, and girl after he finished "D" he looked up at me in such a seductive tone and said; I need my dessert now! OMG! "Pam, what did you do girl"? "What you think I did"? "Girl he started kissing all over me, got down to Pam's Pearl and looked at me and said may I". "Girl, what did you say"? "D," what could I say at that point". "It was more like what was I thinking". "

I said to myself this MF betta not stop! "Girl he is the bomb"! "D" I'm telling you now girl I am not going to be able to see any more of those tricks". "Girl I like me some LB"!

"So what's up on your home front"? "Pam girl Shaun is about the same". "Girl our first encounter was to die for". Details heffa! "Girl he came by Friday and I thought nothing of it because we were just talking shop". "We were in the kitchen and I'm cooking dinner, and girl, Pam he came up from behind and started touching and kissing me seductively. "Ok, "D," what did you have on"? "Girl I had on the boy shorts, and yeah smelling good, hair hanging"! "Okay "D" that explains the attack in the kitchen". "Girl when I knew anything we were on the kitchen floor"! "He had that shit planned Pam, because he turned the stove off". "Anyway, Pam I can see why the brother has ten different baby mamas and 12 kids". "The man is fine as hell and he's good with the reproductive system"! "What about the pearl "D," OMG, girl you know that is a prerequisite when dealing with "D"! "Girl you are crazy". "So what's up with the other tricks"? "You know Pam, I'm feeling me some Shaun, but girl he got too much on his plate". "He can't properly take care of me the way I'm used to being taken care of". "You know how we get down". "Yeah I know". "Girl LB came by the day I moved in and gave me a grand and told me to get what I needed and if that wasn't enough to let him know". "OMG, girl no he didn't"! "Pam you struck gold in every area"! "D" I am feelin him, but I know there is going to be a price to pay somewhere down the line". "He is fine, powerful, and very generous to me". "This type of relationship is unheard of for us to have just hooked up". "D" sometimes I think I'm dreaming". "Well, all I can say Pam is that I wish Shaun were in that position". "All his money goes to his baby mama's fan club"! "Girl you are crazy"! "I mean really Pam; you would think that he would have wrapped up on at least number three; he had twins with her". "Oh no, he had to keep this crazy cycle going". "Really"! "So what are you going to do "D"? "I think I'm going to do him when I want, but Pam I'm not going to lie to you girl, I'm trickin some of these niggas"! "Just be careful "D," I told you what Kenny said that the guys were saying about you". "Yeah Pam you told me, but don't forget what you always say, if we allow our self-worth to be built on what others think of us, it is the beginning of the end". "Remember when we use to cherish people's opinions about us until we tried to pay our bills with their opinions and our shit got turned off". "How about that"! "I'm impressed "D," your wild ass do be listening". "You go girl, but still be careful". "You know I will".

Chapter 10

"Hey "D," girl LB just called me and told me that they had some openings in the bureau". "Like what girl"? "LB said they are looking for some new blood to go into the drug enforcement unit, sex crimes, and precincts detective units". "Pam I thought we had to be on the department for a while before we could even apply for those positions". "D" when you have the kind of power that LB has; you can do what you want". "Is he recommending you"? "Of course, did you have to ask"! "OMG! I'm telling you now Pam, I'm going after rank". "I'm sorry, I am not about to stay in this patrol car and answer calls forever; two years is enough and I'm not waiting another year". "I see the way Captain Roberts looks at me, well it is getting ready to be on". "Wait a minute, I know you are not talking about the Captain Roberts that's married". "You heard me"! "Yes I am". "I know you are not talking". "D," LB is getting a divorce". "Has he got it yet Ms. Pam"? "Well no, but he is in the process of getting it". "Do you have any proof"? "Look "D," I'm not going through this with you". "I know you're not". "I also know that you are hoping like hell that he is not lying to you". "Let me say this to you Pam; word around the precinct is that LB is still with his wife". "I did not want to tell you like this, but we are supposed to be girls". "I'm telling you before you get in to deep and you got time to get out of it unless you are cool with it". "Now if you are cool with it, then please spare me the drama on what I should or should not be doing". "Moving on, I will be in a specialized unit in two months, and that my dear you can take to the bank"! "D" you are a trip". "Call it what you want, it is going down". "Well all I can say is please be careful "D". "Pam, you always telling me to be careful, what about you"? "I know you are in deep "like" with LB, but you better smell the coffee baby; it is what it is". "D" I really do thank you for letting me know what the word is on LB". "Now I just have to figure out how I'm going to deal with it once I find out what is really going on with him". "D," I think I'm in love with him". "Wow"! "Pam it hasn't been long enough for you to be in love with him". "Are you serious"? "Yes, I am and who are you to tell me how long it takes to fall in love"? "He is good to me and I'm at place in my life where I feel this is what I need". "He is just what I want right now". "As a matter of fact, I don't think I am going to dig or snoop regarding his personal life". "What"! "You got to be kidding me Pam". "Nope"! "As you say 'D', it is what it is"! "Most of those who are talking behind my back aren't really concerned they're just gossiping". "Please let us not forget that most of them are jealous, because if LB hadn't asked me out, someone else would have". "Personally, I don't think anyone would have stepped up to the plate and did what he did to save my job". "Yeah, you got a point there".

"Everybody was saying you were not going to make it". (Yeah including you!) "That's what I'm saying". "So with all of that in mind, I'm going to take my chances on me some LB"! "Now how about that"! "All righty then Ms. Pam, you know "Dirty D" got your back whatever road you take". (Whatever, you probably gossiping right with them!) "I'm just saying "D," It don't get no better than this". "Whatever is going on with LB, I can't tell if he is with his wife". "D," he spends at least four nights a week with me". "If he can do that and be married, well I guess she got three nights and I got four". "I can handle that if she can". "I hear you girl". "We'll I tell you what, I don't want Captain Robert's ass four nights a week". "I just want some of that power he has". "I heard downtown was big on listening to him as well". "Yeah I hear LB talking about how he is one of the smart ones they depend on". "He is just not as bold as LB, but just as powerful". "So "D" what's your strategy"? "Girl you know the play, I am not beating around the bush". "The next time I catch him looking at me, I am going to whisper something in his ear". "Girl you a fool"! "No, Pam, this man gazes at me like I'm magic". "For real "D"? "Yes ma'am, it is almost uncomfortable". "Not for me though". "You know how I get down, it's on baby". "OMG"! "D" he not the best looking guy, how are going to deal with that"? "Pam you tripping, I don't care about how this man looks"! "I'm trying to get out of this police car". "D" I know you feel like this is an obstacle, but you shouldn't be frustrated". "Just remain consistent and do everything that is expected of you and you'll see, things will change for you". "Pam please, I know you are not giving me advice on wanting to be around power"! "Girl Boo"! "Yes "D," I'm giving you advice". "Remember the verdict is still out on LB"! "Besides, I told you when I'm advising you, I'm talking to myself as well". "D" we both need to realize that we are dealing with some self-esteem issues; I don't care how smart or cute we think we are". "The way we are going about doing things is not cool". "One day we are going to have to stop running and face ourselves". "Until then Pam, I'm doing me"!

Chapter 11

"Wow "D," it's been three years already"! "We must go and celebrate getting out of that blue crappy uniform". "Yeah baby, I am enjoying wearing my own clothes". "Pam it feels so good to be out of that patrol car answering calls after calls".

"Yeah, you said you were going to do it". "Hold up, do I hear some sarcasm in your voice"? "Please don't judge me Pam, you are in sex crimes unit even with all the trouble you had". "Okay, "D," just be careful". "Why you say that"? "LB told me about you leaving Captain Roberts alone". "That's right and on to the next"! "But Pam, please tell me he didn't tell people his business"? "Girl you know him and LB are thick as thieves". "Yeah, but you wouldn't think a married man would go around and say he's been quit by his mistress". "Really"! "What happened "D"? "Pam he was getting to deep". "I couldn't get off into him like you are with

LB". "I could barely do what I did, but you know a girl has to do what a girl has to do and that patrol car wasn't getting it". "He thought that step up to the detective bureau was going to make me be beholding to him". "I don't think so"! "So now what "D"? "You know the promotion test is coming up so I've been studying like a mad woman". "Me too; LB has been going over some materials with me that will be on the test". "You know we only have a couple of weeks before we have to take it". "Yeah girl, I know". "Guess who I've been studying with"? "Major Rax"! "No "D"! "Girl he is so fine". "I know"! "We can barely get any studying done". "D," tell me you are not sexually involved with him". "I could tell you that I'm not if that's what you want to hear; but if you want the truth, I am and he is awesome"! "How about that"! "OMG "D"! "He is so married and has children"! "Okay, what's your point Pam"? "I'm not trying to fall in love, I like the sex and the power"! "And guess what"? "When this is over with, I am going to be a sergeant after I take this test"! "D" do you know how many women would die to be with him"? "Yeah, but I got him on lock down around here". "What he does at home is between him and his wife; what he does around the department is my business". "I hear you Dirty "D". Can't nobody do it like "D"!

"So what's up with Tyrone and LB"? "They're getting along very well". "I don't like LB sleeping over when Tyrone is here". "He stays late and leaves before Tyrone gets up". "That's cool". "Is LB okay with that"? "Oh my God yeah; he totally respects the fact that I don't have Tyrone around situations like that". "Well your girl doesn't have that problem, and MR stays over a few nights a week. What! I don't know what is going on in his home, and quite frankly I don't care; but girl yes he stays over three and four nights a week. Now I will say this, I can do with him what you do with LB". "I do like me some MR". "OMG "D"! I can't believe you! "You've even given him a nick name"!

"Well believe me baby girl". "I'm playing this out for everything I can get". "When this relationship is over I will be at least a Colonel". "You are serious aren't you"? "Yes I am and ain't nothin gettin in my way"! "Pam I have to get out of here". "I need to get some studying done, alone". "Yeah you betta if you want a high score". "Girl I want a high score, but trust me it is not going to matter". "I guarantee you Pam when the scores come out and the formalities are over, I will be a sergeant". "You know what "D," I believe you girl. but "D" can I let you in on something"? "Go head Pam, since when did you start asking me can you butt into my business"? "Right, anyway, "D" you sound like you are on some type of vengeance". "Is everything alright"? "Yeah I'm cool". "I'm just doing to them niggas what they do to us Pam". "I am not putting all of my emotions into these men and just come out of with a wet ass; I'm getting what's due me"! "D" they don't owe you anything, what do you mean, "what's due you"? "You are

73

making a conscious choice to deal with those men". "Pam why do you always have to see the bad in what I do"? "No baby girl, I am not trying to see bad in what you do, I just want you to see that you don't have to get where you want to go on your back". "OMG! Really Pam"! "Do you really want to go there"? "Yes, "D," I want you to always be conscious about your actions being a self-image thing". "Thank you ma'am, I will keep that in mind and you do the same". "Moving on, let's study and get a high score because even though someone is helping us it will be known that we are not only beautiful women, but smart women as well". "I know that's right Pam".

Chapter 12

"D," girl the scores are back"! "I know, MR just texted me". "Did he say if we were on the list"? "And you know this man"! "Girl I am so nervous". "LB, told me he would call me and give me a run-down of the list and what takes place next". "A bunch of interviews and you know my boy will be on one of the panels". "OMG"! "Girl I am so excited". "I hope LB gets his promotion as well". "You know he is Pam". "I'm just saying". "Let me call you back "D," this is LB". "Okay". "Hi baby". "Hey sweetheart what's up"? "Stop it LB, you know what I want to hear". "I know baby, well you and your girl "D" did the damn thing". "What! What"! "You guys are in the 95 percentile". "That's what I'm talking about baby". "Let me call you right back, got to call my girl "D". "Call me right back Pam so that I can tell you what is next". "My bad baby, how did you do"? "I will talk to you when you finish hollering at "D," okay baby".

Hello "D," girl we are in the 95 percentile"! "That's what I'm talking about". "It is on now baby, rank here we come"! "Girl you crazy"! "D" I told you it would be good if we got a high score so that it wouldn't be hard for them to help us". "Okay you were right". "How did LB do"? "I don't know, he is going to be over later and go over the promotional procedure with me". "How did MR do"? "They don't take test; I think they just go through a series of interviews". "I'm getting ready to see him in a minute". "We got some celebration to do because I am getting ready to become a sergeant"! " Hey"! "Oh, you just know you getting promoted". "Yes ma'am, girl it is about to be on". "Pam I am going to have those little tender-rony officers' at my beckon call". "D" something is seriously wrong with you". "Call it what you want, why don't you just practice calling me Sgt. Crenshaw or maybe I'll let you call me Sgt. "D".

"I'm going to pray for you "D". "Girl you are tripping, you know you feel the same way". "Now you want to act all high and mighty". "No that's not what I'm doing "D". "You acting like nothing matters, people feelings are involved". "When you have people looking up to you and looking at you like a mentor, you have to be careful on how you treat them". "D" some people take how they look up to people real serious". "I know you have heard some disastrous stories on how mentees have been used by the mentors' and they have come back and killed their asses"! "Pam only your ass thinks like that". "I'm just saying "D," you need to be careful when dealing with people's feelings". "Pam let me holler back at you, MR is at the door". "Okay". "Hey baby, congratulations! Thank you baby, this is a cause for a little celebrating". "Yes it is". "You and your girl Pam scores were remarkable". "Everyone is talking about them". "Really"! "What's the scuttle bug"? "They can't believe how high you all scored and they realize that you all will no doubt fall into cluster A". "OMG"! "I am so excited baby"! "So how does your promotion work"? "All we have to do is have a couple of interviews and then the chief and the board of commissioners decides". "How do you feel about it"? "Oh make no mistake about Sgt. Crenshaw, you are getting ready to make love to Lt. Colonel Rax"! "Oh baby, congratulations"! "Thank you baby". "Hold up, did you call me Sgt. Crenshaw"? "Yes I did"! "OMG"! "Baby, how do you know"? "I mean I thought we had to go through some interviews". "You do, but with me in your corner, you know it's all gravy". "Baby I love you"! "D" what did you say"? "I said I love you". "Baby I was hoping you were feeling what I was feeling". "I know I'm married, but I dig the hell out of you". "Dig MR"? "Baby you know I care deeply for you, stop playing". "Come here, kiss me"! All I could do was submit to MR. He made me feel so good all over. He knew just how to seduce me and once he did, it was on. There was nothing MR wouldn't do for me in or out the bed. I must say, I enjoyed him so much that I forgot about all my other discrepancies that I had going on around the department. Somehow I started feeling that as soon as MR helped me to make Sgt., he was going to demand that our relationship becomes exclusive, that is on my part anyway, remember he's married. I cared for him so much that if he asked me I think I would consider. Oh but what do I do about Shaun? Damn I like me some Shaun, even though he has too many damn kids! We'll see what happens because I am determined to become Sgt. Crenshaw by hook or crook!

Chapter 13

"Hi baby, I thought you would never get here". "Hi honey, I had to tie up some loose ends at the precinct". "Where's Tyrone"? "He's at my parent's house". "Did you tell your family about your score's"? "No, I thought I would tell them after I got all of the particulars from you". "Well where do you want me to start"? "Do you want to make love to Captain Levi Brown first, or do you want to know all of the particulars"? "OMG"! "Baby congratulations"! "You know I always want you, but can we talk about the particulars first"? "Yeah girl, I was just kidding about the love-making first but you are talking to Capt. LB"! "Okay, you go boy, I've never made love to a Captain"! "Ooh yeah, let's sees what that's like". "Stop stalling, what's the next step"? "Well you will have to go through a series of interviews and depending on how you score with the panel will depend on what cluster you will be placed in". "The clusters are A-H". "How long is this process"? "It's about two months' worth of interviews and I'm talking with everyone who took the test". "Then what happens when all the interviews are over"? "It's promotion time"! "Girl stop worrying, you know you and "D" are cool". "Ya'll are with the two most powerful men in the department"! "Oh baby I can't wait". "You want to be in uniform or stay in the bureau when you become Sgt. Pamela Greer"? "Oh baby I don't care, I am so excited". "Did MR make it"? "You know he did". "He is Lt. Colonel Rax". "I know "D" is excited about that". "Why did your expression change"? "LB, "D" is doing too much". "Why you say that"? "She thinks she is going to hang out with MR and all the rest of the guys she deals with". "Well I can tell you that MR is not going for it even though he's married". "I tried to tell her that, but she said no married man will ever tell her what she can and can not do"! "She told me that MR and Shaun hate each other and she thinks that is good so it will be easy to do them both". "I tried to tell her that's not a good idea, but telling "D" something sometimes is like pulling teeth". "She's so head-strong and sometimes I think she competes with me". "I know she cares for me like a sister, but when I'm trying to tell her something about various things we are discussing, she acts as if she's mad because I either know more than her about the subject matter or because I have my degree". "I think she thinks I feel like I know more than her". "The craziest thing about all of it is that's not how I feel at all". "To be quite honest with you, I think she is very smart". "Sometimes I think she acts reckless, but even with that she handles herself well and always comes out on top". "I don't know baby, I do worry about her at times". "Okay baby, it's cool to look out for your girl, but she's grown and trust me; she is going to learn how things work around this department, especially with MR". "So much for all of that, I'm ready to get inside of you". "Stop talking like that".

"Like what, I want to lick on my pearl"? OMG, LB was so good with my pearl. He was good with everything, but especially with my pearl. We made love like it was the first time. He was so gentle and of course so good. LB always made me feel like I was special! I could never think of being with anyone else. Every now and again, I would think about what "D" said about LB still being with his wife, but it was always a short thought. LB and I never talked about his situation with her and I was so in love with him that I think I wanted to keep believing what he said. He protected me to a degree that no one could get to me to tell me anything. They all feared him. He even controlled who I partnered with and even they protected me from the rumor mill. The man had it going on! However, the fact remained that he was a married man and deep within that bothered me because of how my mom raised me and of course that good old HB—Holy Bible!

Chapter 14

OMG! It's Friday and promotions are coming out today. I wanted to call "D" and LB, but I thought I would wait on my call. (Phone ringing) I don't know this number, who could this be? I better answer it. "Hello"? "Is this Detective Pamela Greer"? "Yes it is". "Detective Greer this is Lt. Colonel Hudson, I am calling on behalf of the St. Louis Chief of Police to let you know you have been promoted to the rank of Sergeant". "You should report to the command post at noon today". "OMG, thank you so much Colonel Hudson; I will be there". Before I could call "D" or LB, they were both calling me with their good news, or so I thought. I answered the phone putting LB on hold. "What's up Sergeant Crenshaw, I know you got that call". "No girl what are you talking about". "I just got my call and I am Ms. Sgt. Pamela Greer". "What"!

"Congratulations Pam"! "When did they call you"? "I got my call a few minutes ago". "My phone hasn't rang". "Let me call you right back "D," this is LB calling". "Okay, I will call you back, I'm getting ready to call MR, okay". "What's up Sgt. Greer"? "Hi baby, thank you so much, I am so excited". "LB "D" hasn't gotten her call yet". "Oh by the way what about you, did you make it"? "You know I did". "You are talking to Captain Brown"! "Oh baby congratulations"! "Thank you, congratulations to you as well sweetheart, you know I don't except verbal thank you or apologies". "You're so crazy; baby what happened with "D"? "Pam they only had a few openings for Sergeants, so she will be on the next list, but she is being moved to Sex Crimes". "You know what Pam"? "What"? "I also think it is MR way of letting her know he controls shit". "Really"? "Yeah, I've seen him move like this on other situations". "Wow"! "I will see you tonight won't I"? "Of course Sergeant Greer"! "Okay, I will talk with you later; I am going to call "D". "Okay, I will see you this afternoon, down at command post; oh I forgot you will be there, okay see you then". I called "D" but didn't get an answer; I'm assuming she is talking to MR. I started calling everybody I knew to tell them I was now Sergeant Pam Greer. I was so excited I could barely see straight. As I was leaving the house to go to command post, I could hear Mrs. Brooks in the kitchen. I ran in there where she was and told her the good news. She congratulated me and I left the house heading for command post so excited. "D" called me as I was driving downtown. She said the same thing that LB said and was pretty happy for the change and could not wait for the next promotions to come out. After all she was in cluster A and would definitely be with the next group of officers to be promoted. My phone was blowing up as you could pretty much expect it to. I talked to pretty much everyone I cared about and put it on face book for all the haters to gloat! I know I should not feel like that but they were always whispering behind my back. If you looked like anything, you had to be screwing you way to success. What they fell to realize was that "D" and I was in the 95 percent percentile, which meant that we were going to get promoted without any help. Duh! The ceremony they put on down at the Chief's office was not intimate but it was cool. You got sworn in and then given your gold badge. Man I am on cloud nine. I called my dad and told him that I wanted to pick Tyrone up so that I could tell him the good news. Our little service lasted about an hour because we had to go back over to Laclede's division to pick up our uniforms. After I left there it was time to pick up Tyrone. When I walked in the building, he asked me where was Pops. "Hello son, so glad to see you too"! "Oh mom, I just wasn't expecting you, I'm glad to see you too"! Tyrone was getting so tall. He was 10 years old and began to start looking like his dad. As we were walking to the car I told Tyrone I had some good news to tell him. He asked me was

I getting married. I told him know, that I was now Sgt. Mom to him. His eyes got so big and he said, "wow mom, that's awesome and cool"! We went straight to my parents' house and everyone was filled with joy upon our arrival. My mom wanted to cook and my dad thought we should all go out to eat. Needless to say, the plans I had were totally different from theirs. Yep, I wanted to be with my man LB, no "Captain LB"! I could not wait to see him. We all finally came to an agreement that mom would cook. Mom could always put something quick together and it would be like she had it planned. My brother and sister's all came by, which was cool. They were all happy for their baby sister. Oh I forgot to tell ya'll, I'm Detective Sergeant Pamela Greer; I had to pick up a uniform to do special details and to graduate in! I can't wait to get by myself and thank God!

Chapter 15

Well it is Monday morning and I now work eight to four with weekends off. How about that! I called "D" to rub it in, but she didn't answer. I started getting dressed for work thinking about what my mom told me about dressing. She told me to look as though I was the Chief of Police. I put on one of my Chaus suits. It was a silk double breasted skirt suit, with my grey suede Bandolina's 2" pumps. I was smelling good, make up on just right for daytime wear, and my hair down just flowing as I walked. Oh I was so glad I didn't have to wear my hair pinned up. I road in listening to Smokey Robinson thinking to myself how happy I was regarding my life as it was just at this moment. Not only am I a Sergeant, I'm a detective Sergeant. I'm in love with a great guy; my son is doing wonderful in school. What more can one ask for. "D" called me before I made it to work and told me what was going on in her neck of the woods. She said she was pretty happy and she and MR were doing just find. I thought to myself how long was that going to last with what I knew about "D". "D" said everything was going great, but "D" had a passion stronger than gold for moving up in the department. It didn't matter who, what or how she had to go about getting there as long as she made it. So in other words, she could be treacherous. I was really scared for her regarding MR because he had the same demeanor as "D". There were so many rumors and stories about MR that it was crazy and scary. The man didn't play. You would have thought he was GOD, however, "D" thought her stuff didn't stink either, and because she was so gorgeous she thought she was Ms. GOD as well. LB asked me to let her know what she was getting into, but "D" said thanks, I got this. All I could say to her was alright MS. "D," handle your business.

It was time for the department to make more promotions and "D" was on pins and needles. I knew she would make it this time around, but I also knew how she felt about the anticipation. LB called me and told me that she made it, but I wanted her to call me with her enthusiasm as I did her. That was a <u>Great</u> feeling! She called me hollering all over the place. "D" what precinct did they send you to"? "Girl, precinct 7"! I thought OMG! Precinct 7 was known for the men of leisure if you know what I mean. I often wondered how you can have a precinct with all those fine ass men. Was that purposely done? However, I could see "D" going through those guys like animals running through the pastures. Remember I told her what LB said about MR. Well as I predicted, "D" started running through the men in precinct 7. Now what I couldn't understand was that she had to know that MR was going to hear about it. But in "D's" mind MR was married and she was grown. She got away with dating three officers before MR got wind of her routine. I must say she was rocking and rolling. Unfortunately when MR struck, he struck hard. MR went for the guzzler! MR got the three brothers she was dealing with. Two of the guys lost their jobs and one was so deeply buried in what they call mops and brooms, you forgot he was on the department. Did "D" feel any remorse for them? No! It was going to be very interesting to see where this was going to go between "D" and MR. MR sat the officers up and you couldn't tell he had anything to with "D". Rumor had it that it was about "D," but it couldn't be proved. After all the guys saw what happened to the three officers I can tell you they wanted no part of "D". I asked "D" about the rumors, but she swore up and down their issues had nothing to do with her. I asked "D" was she still seeing Shaun and she said he was still around, but they weren't as tight as they were in the beginning. Now Shaun was a pretty smooth guy. He was just as fine as MR, had a lot of class, a Sgt., but just too many babies and no power! What I will say about Shaun is he was not scared of MR and he was very smart. He was promoted to Sergeant with me, but somehow I thought to myself that Brother Shaun was not going to get too much further. Reason being, Shaun was a ladies' man and for whatever reason it appeared that he had a baby with every sister he laid down with. I do believe they were trying to trap him. Shaun didn't care who got pregnant, he was still going to do his thing and take care of his kids. You would think after the 3rd child he would at least strap up. You would also think that the women would only have one, but oh no, some of them had two and three babies by Shaun and knew that he had other baby momma's. I guess they thought they would be the one that could change him. "D" liked him and enjoyed his company, but she wasn't about to get pregnant. I think they both had the same thing in mind. "D" and Shaun had a spark for one another and could hook up at any time as if they never stopped seeing each other. Shaun knew about "D's" relationship with MR and I think that made him want to deal with her that much more. Shaun wanted to let MR know that his power meant nothing to him and just knowing he was dealing with "D" made him feel like he had the power. Everyone knew MR was in love with "D," because she was a Sergeant for maybe a year and half and was then promoted to LT. It took me two years to the day. You know "D" had to let me know she was Ms. Lt. "D" before me. I was cool with it though. We were both smart, beautiful women and deserved to rise to the top. Only I was so scared for "D," but she would always say Pam as long as my courage outweighs my fear, it's okay to be afraid, and by being so relaxed about life in general, that's how I am going to lengthen my life; and then tell me I better take notes, she got this!

Chapter 16

After "D" and I made Lieutenant, the rumor mill was more than I wanted to contend with. "D" on the other hand didn't seem to care because her mission was to be as far up the ladder as she could get. Even though "D" was relatively close with MR, she was just as close to Shaun. I know she was seeing Shaun at least twice a week. MR knew it too. MR hated Shaun, but what kept MR from messing with Shaun is that Shaun knew people along the same rank as MR that was protecting him. Shaun enjoyed the rivalry between him and MR. MR also realized that he had met his match regarding "D". "D" made MR feel so good and he wanted to do whatever it took to keep her happy so she could continue to keep him happy. MR took "D" out of the precinct and put her in a specialized unit thinking that she would not see so many prospects (other officer's) and would slow her role down. Oh he was sadly mistaken. "D" only got worse because of her passion! "D" was able to see all the prominent men in charge. When "D" got downtown; it only made her passion grow stronger. She saw all of the gold bars on their collars and that did if for her. She would call me and say Pam I don't know about you but girl they look so good in their uniform, I can't wait I am going to get some double bars on my shirt real soon. All I could say was you go girl, because "D" had her mind made up. The other ladies we went through the police academy with were still answering calls in the police cars. Of course they called us whores'. We didn't care because we knew we were smart, and they knew it too. They were just envious of us because we kept ourselves up and yeah, we were some gorgeous ladies. "D" was the LT in the Drug Enforcement Unit and the guys in her unit were not too happy about it. What they didn't know was that "D" was smooth as that thing and was just as down with things, if you know what I mean, as the next person. "D" said when she walked into roll call on the first day, of course dressed to kill; she could feel daggers from everywhere. Mostly from people not thinking she deserved to be where she was. "D" loved it! She could give less than a damn and she would give them all a run for their money if they got in her way. What they didn't know is that they didn't want any of "D".

About a month after "D" was in the Drug Unit, they made one of the biggest bust in the history of the Department. "D" being the Lt. of the unit turned in the drugs and money once it was accounted for. The detectives of "D's" unit turned in $3,350,000. 00. "D" and I had always heard that all the drug money that various specialized units got off the streets was not always turned in. I told you all that "D" had more nerve than a toothache, for whatever reason, "D" had the notion to take 50,000. 00. In her mind they were not going to miss it. When she told me that, I bout fell over. I could not believe she did that, by herself. Now remember I also told you all that the detectives counted the money five times before turning it in because that was the procedure. While at roll call the Chief of Detectives was giving everybody their kudos's on their arrest and with his announcement, he said how much was confiscated because it was the largest ever. When those detectives heard the amount, they almost choked. When roll call was over Detective Martin went up to "D" and asked her out to lunch to discuss some things. "D" was fine with it because she had no idea Martin was on to her. They met at Culpeper's in the Central West End. Det. Martin didn't beat around the bush at all. "D" said before the waiter came to get their order he went straight for her throat. "Lt. Crenshaw, I heard you were good and all, but we must have counted that drug money six or seven times, and each time we came up with $3,350,000. 00". "The Chief said $3,300,000.00". "That's $50,000.00 short". "What's up with that"? "Me and the guys are down, but we are down together". "No one person gets a stash to themselves". "Depending on the bust, depends on how much we split, evenly". "Also, we don't make a hit every time we bust someone". "D" said she must have turn beat red. She could not believe Det. Martin had the balls to come to her. After all, everyone knew who she was connected to. However, she responded to him and said okay, my bad. "Det. Martin replied back, my bad"! "Lt. you need to give me 30,000. 00 of that bust money". "D" said she couldn't get any redder, and all she could say was okay, that's fair. She advised him where to meet her later that night. Det. Martin was so bold, he told her that he would prefer that after they finish eating lunch he would like for her to get it for him then. Again, all she could say was okay. I guess both of them were glad to have cleared the air. This type of fiasco went on for about four years after Det. Martin put "D" on game. "D" must have stashed a half a million easily. I asked "D" what she was thinking going along with Det. Martin stealing drug money, with or without him. "D" turned and looked at me and said "look Pam, I'm not about to work around all these motherfuckers and watch them get paid and go home with a "fucken" paycheck that don't amount up to shit for all the shit we take". "I'm going to get mine". "Now you can be Ms. Polly Pure Bread and go home with just a paycheck, but not me baby". "D" what if you get busted, then what"? "That's the chance I am willing to take". "Besides Pam, I heard LB has had his time where he got in on the take as well". "How do you think you get your bills paid"? Now I was turning beet red. "What do you mean"? "Don't play stupid with me; you know exactly what I mean". "While you are playing house and are so in love, LB was living just as happy at his house with his wife". The reason why he is able to get out of the house and spend the night with you is because he was telling his wife he had to work late on several homicides and drug bust. I could not believe "D" was going there with me. I asked her what was up with all the information she seem to have regarding my man and how long had she been keeping all of this from me. I thought we were cooler than that but I see that since I was talking to her about stealing drug money, she felt she had to check me on something. She finally said "I just thought you should know what was going on with LB because it appears that you think he is leaving his wife and he's not". "You need to move on with someone you can call yours, it has been damn near ten years and you are always telling me to focus on where I want to go and not on my challenges, well what about you, are you taking your own advice? Wow! Now "D" couldn't have put that any better than she did. I just didn't like how she came off with her information. She should have told me all that when she found out, my friend, umm. Instead she waits until she gets mad and wants to play that tit for tat game. It's cool, because I thought to myself, bitch you got one coming.

Chapter 17

I sat for a minute and tried to consume all that "D" said. OMG, it was very overwhelming. I didn't know what I was going to say to LB when we got together. I had to prepare myself because he knew me so well he would be able to tell that something was going on with me. I really didn't know how to dissect this information. There were times in the course of our relationship that I saw signs that LB and his wife were doing better than he had led me to believe, but of course I ignored it because his relationship with his wife did not affect me, I was getting what I wanted and doing what I wanted to do. The issue for me now is how I'm going to deal with this information, how am I going to deal with this ten year lie! Do I confront him with the fact that I know him and his wife are doing fine, or do I continue to ignore it? I'm thinking, I can't see him tonight. My mind is wondering so fast and my anxiety level is so high I don't know how to even calm myself down. I know I need to go to the gym to work out for a while to calm myself down. That always seems to do the trick when my anxiety level is on high. I think I will tell LB that Tyrone is not feeling well and I am going to spend the night at my mom's house because she doesn't want him out of bed. He knows mom and dad spoils him so he won't think anything about me staying over there.

OMG I'm so glad it is the weekend and I don't have to work today. I still feel overwhelmed, but I will make it through this BS. I'm thinking about how I should handle this because promotions come out in about two weeks and I want to be a captain. I don't think I give a damn about what LB is doing at this point. At this point in our relationship, he is going to pay for what he values, and that is me. So needless to say, I am going to deal with the bastard until I make at least one more promotion. That shit "D" said to me only gave me more strength to move forward. She wants me to end this relationship with LB, but that would be professional suicide. What is she thinking? I've got to come up with a plan real quick. I am going to work him like he has never been worked before. He thinks he has the game and gone, but oh no, it is about to go down. I am going to need some ammunition against him when I let him go. Reason being is because his ego is going to be effected; he is coming after my ass. I know how to play this game because I've watched him fuck so many people in the ten years that I have been with him. I think I'll start with getting promoted first. After I get promoted to captain, I will start cheating on him. Well I wouldn't call it cheating; after all I am the one that's single. LOL!

I have been talking to Leon Blanks, as a friend, but I know he's interested. Most of them are scared to talk to me because of LB. Leon is about the only who might not be scared. I don't know, but I am about to find out. Leon is a tall, slender brother that thinks he is all of that. He is always talking about having his own business and he is not going to do twenty years on the force. He isn't married and don't have any children, whew! I am not trying to be a stepmother. LOL! I know; I got some nerve! Promotions are around the corner. I can't wait! I know "D" is going to be ringing my phone. She and I haven't talked since she told me about LB. Ring, ring, ring, Speaking of the devil, this is her. "Hey girl what's up"? "You know promotions are out according to MR and I heard you were on the list". "Really"? "You mean LB didn't tell you"? "I haven't talked to him yet". "I was over to my mom house with Tyrone, he had the flu". "Oh, how is feeling now"? "He's good, but you know my mother, she wants to keep him over here where she feels his rest will not be disturbed". "Oh yeah I know how your parents feel about their grandson". "Have you talked to LB about what I said to you"? "We've talked, but not about that". By the way Pam, I'm sorry how that came out. "It's cool "D". "No Pam, it's not cool, I could have told you that much better and sooner than I did; but you caught me at a moment that I couldn't take any more of your goodness". "It's cool "D". "I'm okay and I do understand where you are coming from". (Boo you got one coming baby, you and LB). "Hold on "D," let me get this call". "Hello"? "Hello Lt. Greer, this is Lt. Colonel Johnson calling from the command post". "Hi sir". "Lt. Greer I'm calling to congratulate you on your promotion to Captain". "It will be effective on Monday". "You are to report to the command post where the Chief of Police will be swearing in everyone who got promoted". "OMG"! "Thank you so much LT. Colonel Johnson". "You're welcome; I will see you on Monday morning". (Clicking back over to "D"). "D" girl that was the call"! "What call Pam"? "My promotion"! "Right on girl, congrats"! "Thank you girl". "Well you know I got to go and tell my family". "Okay, call me later". "Will do". "How she like me now"?

Her life changes once she owns' it!

Chapter 18

The word is out that I am now a captain of the Police Department. "D" and LB got promoted about a month before me. My family is so proud of me and others don't understand how I made it. Oh well! I have to call my parents.

"Mom I just got promoted; I am so excited I don't know what to do". "Well baby girl you should be and we are proud of you". "Thanks mom". "Just continue to treat people right and remember to reach back and you will come out on top". "I know mom, you and dad have always taught us to do right by people". "Mom I got to make a move with my personal life that may cause some havoc to my career". "What's going on Pam"? "Well you know LB is married but has always led me to believe that he was getting a divorce". "Now I must admit it has been ten years and no divorce, but because of the way he treats me I kind of ignored the fact that

107

he was still married". "What do you mean Pam"? "Well mom he stays over like he's single so I kind of thought that he must not be with her". "When he's not with me he's at where I thought was his apartment". "I have been over where he says is his place and it looks like a bachelor's place". One day "D" and I had a big argument and she told me that LB and some of the other married men on the department share an apartment and make women think they live by themselves". "OMG Pam, are you serious"? "Yes ma'am". "Baby you know you are going to have to confront this situation and deal with the outcome". "I know mom, but you can bet there is going to be a negative outcome". "Why Pam"? "He is probably going to feel like he has done so much for me so I owe him". "That's how they think around the police department mom". "Once someone does something for you it's on, you almost owe them your life". "Pam that's not what I taught you baby". "I know mom, but I am just going to be honest, I got caught up in the game". "I know this is not going to be easy so I'm letting you know that I am going to have to lean on you". "Please don't tell dad, he would be ashamed of me". "No he would understand sweetheart, what he would want to do is kill LB". "You know Pam, we really liked him". "I would have never thought he would turn out to be that type of man". "Mom I think he's a good man, I think he just want his cake and want to eat as well". "Well God would not like that and karma is going to get him". "You just make sure you get out of this mess". "You are a beautiful, smart young lady and you have everything going for you". "You don't have to be second to any woman". "I know mom, thank you so much for listening". "I'm getting ready to go home and I know LB is going to be over there because of the promotion". "Okay keep me posted honey". "Can Tyrone stay over for the weekend"? "You know you don't have to ask that sweetheart". "Oh Pam, you know I will be cooking a big dinner on Sunday to celebrate". "I know mom". "I will be there at 3:00pm". "Okay baby talk with you later". "Okay love you mom".

Well I guess I got to put on my game face because it is about to go down. When LB comes over I am going to be ready for his ass. Who does he think he is lying like a rug to me? He could have told me the truth about his wife, that's my decision to make rather I want to continue to deal with him. Speaking of that lying son of a bitch, this is him. "Hello"? "Hi baby, I hear congratulations are in order". "Thank you sir"! "Well I guess you know a celebration is in order as well". "Yes I do know that". "I am going to go out with a few friends and celebrate tonight". "Oh really"? "Yes, a couple of friends that I went through the academy with and a few that I met along the way want to take me out". "Oh, okay". "I will call you LB when I get freed up and then we can talk". "Okay baby, I'll talk with you later". OMG! I know he knows something is up with me, but good that what he needs. I am going to get him like no other has. When a brother thinks he got it going on like LB does, rejection can be a motherfucker. I'm going to see how powerful he is in one minute. I think I will start by not going home. This is going to be good. I am going to see where Leon head is as well. Wow, every time I speak someone's name they seem to call me. Ring, Ring…"Hey Leon, what's up"? "Congratulations baby". "Thank you". "What's on your agenda tonight"? "I'm going out with a couple of friends that I went through the academy with and some I met along the way". "Why what's up"? "Oh I wanted to take you out for a dinner to celebrate if that's alright with you". "Okay, but I've made arrangements to meet them tonight, are you free tomorrow"? "Yes that works for me". "Okay, what time"? "Is six good for you"? "That's cool, I need your address". "Okay, I'll text it to you". "Okay baby, I look forward to seeing you tomorrow". "I wonder what's up with Mr. Leon". "I heard he is a smooth talker, but I got something for that ass as well. He is in for a rude awakening. Well I shouldn't say that, he could be genuine. After all, at least he's not married! Let me see, what am I going to wear tonight? It's got to be good because I am going to see some of the people I went through the academy with that I have not seen in years. I am so glad I didn't pick up weight like Sonja did. She is 6'9" and heavy through the middle. OMG! Her promotion did her in. She got lazy and just started eating and sitting. When I was in the precinct with her I tried to get her to workout with me, but she said girl you know I didn't like that shit in the academy, what makes you I want to do now that I don't have to? Anyway, that's on her. Oh yeah, this is it. This is hot! Another one of my LBD's baby! Let me just turn on some jazz, have a glass of wine, and get dressed. I got a couple of hours before I leave. I need some time to sort some things out. I have got to find the right time to let LB have it baby. I think I want to give it to him like no other has and I don't mean sexual! He won't be expecting me to let him go. I know he knows something is up, but baby when he realizes that I'm leaving his ass alone—Whew! I guess I will continue to get dressed to my all-time favorite, Temptations, and then leave for the evening.

Chapter 19

Well the night is still young and it was nice seeing everyone. Some were genuine and others were full of shit, but oh well. That's power for the course. I wasn't ready to go in and I must admit; I was feeling Mr. Leon. Even though it's late, I think I will text him. (Texting) What's up baby, are you still up? Would you like to have a night cap before turning in? (Leon) Wow, I sure would. You want me to come to you or you to me? (Me) Me to you if that's okay. (Leon) That's cool, my address is 2222 Lindell Pl. See you in a bit. OMG! Why did I do that? I got my LBD on looking hot as that thang, smelling good as that thang, and hairstyle off the chain. I know this man is going to want to be all over me. Oh well! I'm rolling in my Benz listening to my boy Smokey Robinson, getting all in the mood. It might be on tonight. Knock, Knock, "Just a minute". "He is probably getting himself together because it is after 2:00am in the morning". "Hey baby"; "hi Leon". "You guys just finished partying"? "Yes and I wasn't ready to turn in". "Oh, so what did you have in mind, sexy lady"? "I must say you look absolutely stunning". "Why thank you Leon". "You look good at 2:00am in the morning yourself". "Did I wake you"? "No, I was going over a business prospect, I'm good". Leon always wanted people to think he was a businessperson and was not going to do twenty years on the force; whatever! "I'm glad you called". "Why is that"? "Pam you know I'm interested in you, but word on the streets is that you were LT. Colonel LB's woman and I didn't want to get into that". "Leon I am my own woman". "How about that"! "Lt. Colonel Brown is a married man". "Okay baby, I just needed clarity". "Now that you have clarity what's up"! "What do you want to be up"? "Leon at 2:00am in the morning, what do you think I want"? "Baby I don't want to assume anything and I don't want you for the night; I want to get to know you". "Trust me Pam; I want you tonight like you wouldn't believe baby, but much more than that". "Okay Leon, that's fair but I'm just going to be honest with you, I'm feeling you and I want you to kiss me all over baby". "Wow! It's like that baby"? "Yes it's like that, now are you up for the task"? "I do believe I am Ms. Pam". "You don't beat around the bush do you"? "No I don't, it is what it is". Leon had some jazz playing low and offered me some wine. We sipped and talked for about an hour about the job and his personal goals. I got tired of the small talk and just told him to do me! The look on his face was overwhelming. Men always act like they got game, but when a woman bring it to them bold, they are lost for words. Leon started doing his thing and OMG, did he know what he was doing? When Leon got to Pam's pearl he about blew me away. I went into a zone like I had never gone to before. Umm, was I horny or was he really good? I thought LB was the bomb, oh boy! After it was all done there was no way I could get up and go home. He whispered to me would I please stay over. I looked at his fine ass and said; "I couldn't leave if I wanted to baby". "Why is that"? Leon I literally feel like this is where I should be". I knew he was going to want to talk. See ya'll, that's the insecurity in men. Whenever you tell them something pertaining to sex, they always ask you a dozen questions. If they knew who they were and what they were doing they could tell by your reactions if they were any good. "Baby let's talk in the morning over a cup of coffee". "That's cool, good night baby".

OMG! I could not believe this man, he woke me up kissing all over me, again stopping at Pam's Pearl, and you know the rest is history. I told him I have not felt like that in a while. And like any man would, he asked me felt like what? Are we going to go through this again? "Baby let's get up and shower and have some coffee and talk". "That's a good ideal baby". "I like shower action, lol". Of course he wanted to get busy in the shower, but I told him I thought we needed to discuss some things. The way he made me feel, I could have gone another round with the brother. He was cool; we showered together and then got dressed. I had to wear one of his big tees, because remember, all I had was my LBD! Of course I had a workout outfit in my gym bag which I always kept in my car that Leon went to get it for me. He got the coffee ready and made some breakfast. OMG! He can cook too! All I can say to ya'll is that the night was amazing!

We talked as we ate breakfast about having a relationship, but that wasn't the issue. My issue was how was I going to break it off with LB? Leon knew I was still dealing with LB because no one had ever moved up in the department the way that "D" and I did without help. I don't know why I felt this was going to be hard with the way LB has been lying to me. But something in me still wanted to be with him. Oh I know what I can do, I can do both of them. Men do it all the time. That's what I'll do. Most men that have their own spots usually like for their women to stay over with them. Leon seems like that type. I'm going to go for it even if it doesn't last long.

I couldn't wait to call my girl "D," even though I owed her an ass kickin. "What's up "D"? "Hey Pam, girl I enjoyed myself last night". "Did you see how some of them let themselves go"? "Yes I did girl". "So Ms. Pam where did you go last night because I called you when I got in the car and this morning and your phone went to voice mail". "Girl I went over to Leon's house". "What"! "Okay, give me all the 411; how was that fine ass motherfucker"? "Girl all the female officer's want a piece of that ass"! "Well tell them all to back the fuck up, because he's mine"! "Yours???? Yep! "D" didn't know that I knew she was pushing up on Leon. "So what's up with you and LB"? "What do you mean what's up with me and LB"? "We're still cool". "They do two so guess what, it is about to go down". "I am doing them both". "I can't believe you are asking what about LB". "You do more than one all the time, why can't I"? "You can, I just thought you were so in love with LB". "I still love LB in spite of what you said about him". "I just want to explore other opportunities". "Okay my sister, I hear yah"! "So how was Mr. Leon"? "Girl for a minute I thought I was in orbit". "No Pam, is it like that girl, it's like that "D"! "Did he hit the pearl"? "Girl please, you know that's a prerequisite for us"! LOL! "You crazy Pam"! "No, I'm real"! "So what's your next step with him"? "Well "D," the cool part about this is I really enjoyed being at someone else's spot". "He is clean; I mean his place was to die for". "'D' his bed was so comfortable girl I didn't want to get up"! "The black satin sheets were to die for". "I was so amazed by his hospitality, and I'm going back for more". "I heard that". "Now Pam let's get down to the nitty gritty, what are you going to do about LB". "I am going to play him like he plays everybody else". "Pam you got to be careful". "You know they think their shit doesn't stink and they can do to others, but you are supposed to just take their shit". "I know; I got a game plan for that ass". "What do you have up"? "I need to get my ammunition out "D". "Do you think I was with this motherfucker for ten or is it eleven years and don't have ammo on his ass". "I'm just going to be honest with you Pam, I didn't know what you were thinking hanging out with his lying ass for that many years anyway". "Well I'm a captain huh"? "To be quite honest with you "D," so far I've had a sweet career and the ten years wasn't so bad either". "Yeah, I must say, we have got it going on". "We'll all I have to say to you is to be careful and if you need me I'm here". "Okay, I appreciate you"! She is so full of it. I am going to get that ass too! She don't care what happens to me for real, she probably wants Leon. She don't know I know she gave him a hard time when he worked for her because she couldn't get him to succumb to her

BS. Leon got promoted and left her precinct and went in the bureau of investigations to another precinct. She thought she was so cute and all put together that everybody wanted her high yellow ass! Not! Leon is mine honey! Let me text LB, I know he is wondering where I am. (Text) High baby, you know I miss you and I can't wait for you to taste your pudding! That ought to get him to respond!

Chapter 20

Ring, Ring, Oh good this is LB. "What's up baby, I was wondering when you were going to be by to get your pudding and take me to the moon". "Sorry, Ms. Greer, he won't be taking you to the moon today"? "Who is this"? "This is Mrs. Lt. Col. Levi Brown". OMG! "This is Captain Pamela Greer; what can I do for you". "You can tell me why you are texting my husband obscene messages"? "You must have the wrong number ma'am". "No Capt. Greer, I don't have the wrong number, I have been reading your text to my husband for a while and it needs to stop". OMG! I didn't know what to say or do. My heart was palpitating so fast, I thought I would die. "Mrs. Brown I don't know what you are talking about". "Yes you do and I want to meet with you young lady". "I need for you to meet with me at the Café' O's in the Chase Park Plaza today in two hours".

"Mrs. Brown I don't think we need to speak with each other, I told you I think you are mistaken me for someone else". "Ms. Greer, I will see you in two hours and I suggest you don't be late, or I will be going to IAD". "Oh and by the way, no need to look for your LB, because he is indisposed right now".

OMG! I have to call "D". Ring. . . Ring…"What's up Pam"? "D" you will never believe what just happened to me". "Damn I just got through talking to you, what happened". "Girl LB's wife just called me". "You lying"! "No and she is demanding me to meet her at Café O". "No shit"! "No shit"! "Are you going"? "She told me I better be there in two hours or she is going down to IAD". "Can you meet me there"? "Hell yeah, you know I got your back". I was still pissed at "D" for the way she came to me about LB but I could always count on her to have my back. "Okay I will see you there". "Oh and "D," sit at the bar where we always sit and bring one of your boy toys so she don't get suspicious". "You know how you do it". "Girl you crazy, but okay I'll see you shortly". "Thanks "D". Well I know what I'm not wearing, my LBD! I got jokes at a time like this! You know I never could understand how a cheating brother could leave texts from his mistress in his phone. All one has to do is take the memory card out of a phone and stick it in a computer and get all the information they want. I mean brothers think they are so smart and really they are so damn dumb. I am thinking that's how Sister Brown figured this shit out. But I can't understand why LB is not answering his phone? Damn I should have listened to my mother! I haven't really talked to him since my promotion and I know he knows I have not been home nor over to my mom's house. LB was known to do drive byes to see where I was when he wasn't with me. Brothers are known to try to control two households, but at this point in my life, I was done being controlled. Well it's about that time. I put on some nice jeans, a sweater top and some low heels because I didn't know if I was going to have to get in the trenches with Mrs. Brown. I jumped into the Benz and turn on me some Maze. I thought I would try LB one more time, but still got no answer. I called him on his private line at the precinct and got no answer there. I even told "D" to call MR to see if he knew where he was, but she couldn't get in touch with him either. I thought that was a bit strange but needless to say I continued on. I smelled a rat, but I'm going to deal with it! I pulled up and saw Mrs. Brown's Jaguar. I don't know if she realized that I knew who she was on sight, but I did. Me and my girl "D" checked that out early on in this relationship. I parked opposite of her, got out of car and proceeded into the restaurant. There she was sitting there dressed nice, cute in the face, but thick in the waist. The look on her face was a look of death, just waiting. I could see my girl "D" over in the corner with one of her boy toys having lunch. We nodded the acknowledgement and I walked over to where LB's wife was sitting. I extended my hand out and said "hello Mrs. Brown"; "I'm Pam". She said in a nasty tone, "I know who you are". I sat down wondering OMG, this is not good. "What can I do for you Mrs. Brown"? "For starters you can stop messing with my husband Ms. Pamela Greer". "Who do you think you are in the first place"? "Would you want someone to date your man"? "Well first off Mrs. Brown, that's not how this got started". "When your husband approached me; he said he was in the process of a divorce". "Now granted I didn't check to see how the process was moving alone, but the way he was moving, I thought he was at least separated". "Well no Ms. Greer, he is not separated from me nor are we divorcing". "Well all I can do is apologize for my part in this and assure you that I will not see your husband again". "I would appreciate that very much young lady and thank you for meeting me on such short notice". "You're welcomed". She immediately got up and left. I sat there and wondered what just happened. I could not believe that I had just got confronted by the man I have been dating for ten years, wife. Unbelievable! I didn't know how I felt at that moment; all I know is that it wasn't good. I kept thinking and the thought came to me I don't think I would want to talk to my man's side woman or my husband's mistress; for what? "D" sent her boy toy on his way and came over to my table. She looked at me and said, "Pam you don't look so good". "D," I don't feel good about this at all". "I mean I can't believe I allowed myself to deal with this man for all these years and not demand that he showed me some divorce papers or something". "Pam, remember he took you over to his apartment and I think that gave you some comfort". "D," you knew that whole thing was a facade, and you let me continue on, and you are supposed to be my girl". "I mean really "D"? "Pam there have been times that I have said things to you and you snap off saying that you are irritated". "You talked about how good your man was and how much he loved you; if I had said something to you, you would have automatically thought I was hating on you". "Come on now, really"! "D" how could you say that"? "Because that is what you do Pam". "You go ghost and it's not because you are mad at me, I know that, it's because you trying to deal with your mess". "But "D," you of all people can come to be about anything". "No way would I have thought that coming from you". "Well I'm sorry Pam I didn't tell you earlier, but you seemed so happy and I didn't want to come between you and LB". . "Okay, that's cool; it is what is at this point". "So Pam, what are going to do"? "I got to talk to LB, but in my heart, I'm done with him". "How dare he put me in a situation like this"! "No fore warning or anything". "I can't believe his shit is that raggedy"? "What if she had gotten belligerent with me"? "This can't be happening to me "D". "Life is going so great". "I've been on the force for 11 years, I'm a Captain of Sex Crimes, my son is junior in high school and doing well, and I have my master's degree". "How could I be caught up in such a mess"? "Where did I go wrong"? "All I know is that I must redefine the nature of LB and my relationship".

Chapter 21

Wow! It's been two days and I have not heard from LB. Knock, Knock. "Come in". "Hi baby"! "OMG"! "LB in the flesh"! "Well Sir, where have you been"? "Pam baby just let me explain". "Yeah you got a lot of explaining to do". "Pam she got all the records from my phone, she even got pictures of us baby". "What"! "Yes baby, someone got to her and told everything". "LB I don't care what somebody told her, I'm tripping off the fact that you have lied to me from day one of this relationship". "This relationship has been a lie for eleven long years". "My parents and my son care so much for you and you would have me living a lie like this"? "Baby I can explain, but I don't think this is neither the time nor place to talk about this". "Why not LB"? "Everybody knows about how your wife threatened me about you". "Why you want to be secretive now"? "Pam I'm sorry that you had to go through all of that; please let me make that up to you". "Are you serious LB"? "You think there is a chance for you and I"? "Don't count on it partner"!

"Check this out LB, you want to be treated like a priority, but you treat others like they're an option". "All this time I fell right into your zone". "But this is the truth; not anymore baby, I will expose you for the man you really are if you come after me". "Just like your wife threaten to do me". "You see just like she got pictures of us, I got more than pictures baby". "I got movies of us". "Now fuck with me if you want too". "Pam that's not fair". "Not fair, what's not fair is to tell a bold face lie about what is going wrong in your relationship with your wife, when she is doing right by you". "That's what's not fair motherfucker".

"What kind of man would you have been without a badge"? "You have walked over so many people it is unbelievable". "People who just didn't want to be in your web of BS"! "You literally stole people's career from them". "I'm done with you"!

"Pam what's up with you"? "Let's just say I have awakened". "I was in a deep sleep; no more baby". "I'm not scared of you, I tried to be a good woman to you, but oh no you had to keep lying". "Pam don't end us like this baby". "Why not LB"? "You think I can't do life without you"? "Well guess what; If I run into an obstacle, it's not the end of the world". "If I run into a wall, I'll just turn around, climb over it, go through it, but somehow baby you can believe I will get to my destination without you". "You can best believe dear, it's a rap for you and me". "Now please leave my office". "Baby can I see you tonight"? I don't think so"! LB left looking like a sick puppy. The one good thing LB taught me that I must remember is to focus on where I want to go and not on fear, if I have the courage to begin something, I have the courage to succeed. I must thank him for that lesson and at the same time I'm going to overcome his ass! I know LB is coming back with a vengeance. I have seen how he performs when people get on his bad side.

I need to call my mom because I am going to need extra prayer. I'm not ready to talk to her just yet. Let me call "D". "What's up "D"? "What it do Pam"? "Girl you would not believe who just left my office". "Girl no, not LB; yes LB in the flesh baby". "What did you say, hell what did he say"? "Girl a bunch of BS". "You know, what else was he going to say". "He knew that bitch was coming for me and didn't have the decency to give me a heads up". "She must have spooked the shit out of him". "Pam what did that motherfucker have to say for himself"? "Girl the usual, I'm so sorry type of shit"! "D" girl I let him have it baby"! "It's a done deal". "Pam you are going to have to watch your back". "Yep, and I am prepared". "Girl I learned a lot from his ass in eleven years". "He can come after me if he wants to its going down". "Pam you know it's all over the precincts". "Girl I don't care who knows". "I am so glad to be free of this type of relationship I don't know what to do". "So what's up with you and Leon"? "Now he is who I want to sit down and explain this crap to". "I haven't talked with him yet, but I know he knows". "You told your mom yet"? "Nope, I'm not ready to hear about the religious part of it, and I really am saddened by this whole ordeal". "I kind of need some time to think and some space". "Okay, I understand, you know you can call me anytime". "I know, thanks for listening and for being there for me". "No problem girl, I'll holler"!

Well I guess I'll have to give old "D" a pass now that she has really shown me she was sorry. But I must call my boy Leon. I know how news travels around here and I really want him to hear it from me. I'll call my mom later, or just go over and have one our up all night talks. I love those talks with my mom, they are so rejuvenating. She knew how to make me feel when I was down. I guess I could call her and prepare her for one of our staying up all night flings. She'll like it. "Hi mom, hey baby what's up, what's up, look at you, you think you are so cool". "You taught me". "Okay, anyway, I think we need to have our mom and daughter talk tonight". "Okay, are you okay, I got some time now if you need me". "No mom, I can wait until tonight, I don't want any interruptions". "Okay, baby, I'll be here". "Okay mom, see you later". Okay I need to call Leon now. "Hi baby, hey Ms. Pam, what's up"? "Can you get away for lunch"? "I sure can for you baby". "Can you meet at down at the Central West End at Culpeper's"? "Yeah baby, is everything okay"? "Yes, I just need to talk to you". "Okay see you in twenty, that's cool". I told my Lt. that I was gone for day and left out. As I was leaving I saw LB and MR in the corridor talking. As usual, I was looking good and smelling good. I simply walked by the two as if I didn't know them. I could tell they were discussing our situation, but who wasn't. I got on the elevator with a group of others so I knew he wasn't going to try to talk to me. I got to Culpeper's and Leon had already gotten a table and was waiting for me. He was suited down, looking good as usual. He was in a Sergeant in the Vice Unit and was always dressed nice. OMG! The brother was all of that and some. He always smelled good. If I didn't know any better I would have thought that he and LB shopped together!   (LOL, I still got jokes)! Leon got up like the gentleman he was and pulled my chair out so I could be seated. He looked at me, kissed me on the cheek, and said, "you look sad baby, what's wrong". "Leon I wanted to tell you what was going on before you heard anything, but you know how quick bad news get around in this place". "Yeah baby I heard a little about it". "I don't even want to know what you heard; I just want you to listen". "Long story short Leon, it's over between me and LB". "That's all I need to know baby, I don't need details". "The rumor mill is always negative". "Pam I believe in you and I know who I am". "I'm not tripping off of any of them, but I must say it is amazing as to how much power you have over these people". "How is it that they can be in your business like that and have time to pay attention to their own lives"? "I sometimes wonder about these people, all they do is throw salt on people". "That's what my granny would say". "You got jokes"? "No baby, let's not worry about what they say, let's keep it moving and enjoy life". "I am truly with that"! "As a matter of fact let's toast to that"! "What's up with you this evening"? "I was going over to talk with my mom, why what did you have up"? "I would like to make you a hot bubble bath, make you dinner, and then kiss all over my body". "Your body, oh it's your body now". "We doin it like that"? "Yes we are, if it is okay with you". "I want you to be my lady Pam"! "I want to show you how you should be treated, and not hidden". "You are far too smart and beautiful to be hidden". "Thanks Leon, you don't know how much that means to me; but baby can I take a rain check on tonight, I really want to talk to my mom". "Of course Pam, you just call me when you're ready, I'm patient and you are worth waiting for".

Chapter 22

I could not wait to get to my mom. I knew she was going to have my little favorites and a strong pot of coffee. I loved talking to my mother. She just simply told it like it was. Oh and she had a box of Kleenex as well. There was going to be some tear shedding for sure. I think my dad new about the things me and mom talked about, but he never let on that he knew. He would just treat me like his spoiled baby girl who could do no wrong. Mom was gentle with me, but she told me the truth.

"Hi mom, hi baby, I got your favorite snacks and the coffee is brewing". "Thanks mom, you are something else and I wouldn't trade you for the world". "I wouldn't trade you either baby". "So what's going on in your world Captain Pamela Greer"? "Mom you are not going to believe what happened to me". "What baby"? "Mom, LB's wife approached me"! "What"! "Yeah mom she insisted on me meeting her at a restaurant". "What did you do Pam"? "I met her mom". "What"! "Are you crazy"? "Calm down mom, she wasn't violent and I had "D" to meet me there as well". "Girl, that was not safe". "I know mom, but let me make a long story short for you". "You all will not be seeing LB anymore". "Mom he lied to me"! "He told me he was going to divorce her and come to find out; they weren't having any problems at all". "I spent eleven years with him mom and he never intended to leave her". "I am so disappointed in myself mom". "What are people going to think about me"? "Well first of all baby, we are not going to worry about what people are thinking". "You need to worry first and fore most what God is thinking". "And second of all, those people have a set of issues of their own". "Your issues just stop them from thinking about their own issues". "This is deeper than the people you seem to be worried about". "Pam you have got to do some soul searching sweetheart". "You have got to take some responsibility for what has happened". "What part did you play"? "Did you ever ask him after the first year what was going on in his marriage"? "No mom, things were so good; I never tripped off of asking him". "So you see baby this is not all his fault". "You played a huge role in this saga". "Mom, don't mom me". "You know I am going to give it to you straight". "Pam, I saw your life changing". "I saw all the promotions and how fast they were coming". "I even asked your brother how you were moving so fast when it took him ten years just to make Sergeant and you are a Captain and only been on for ten". "I let that go because I was okay with LB helping you". "I had no idea that he was married with the way he was coming around here". "I know mom, I am so sorry about that". "I did not want to involve you and dad in this mess". "I don't know what to say to Tyrone". "He is old enough to know when things are not right". It's okay baby, Tyrone is also going to learn that emotions play a big role in one's life". "Your dad is doing a good job with him". "He will be okay and he doesn't need to know any details".

"Pam, sweetheart, emotions can take you out if they are not dealt with properly". "Emotions are very dangerous baby; they will also often time cause people not to play fair even if they are the ones doing wrong". "Yeah baby, people don't like being caught up in their own mess and more importantly they don't like being called out"! "Mom how can you create a bunch of turmoil and when it slaps you in the face you want to fault others"? "I don't get it mom". "Don't try baby, you will wear yourself out". "It's call the game of life and people don't always play fair". "Like I said before, people have a problem being called on the carpet with their mess". "I have a book you need to read Pam, other than your Bible; it's called the Four Agreements, by Luis Miguel". "Sweetheart it is one the best books I have read regarding how to deal with people, other than my Bible". "Mom you are something else, you should have been a comedian". "Girl I'm trying to make your pain a little easier". "I know you are hurting". "Eleven years is a long time to be with someone and to have it ripped right from under you must be devastating". "Mom, I met this guy". "No Pam, it is much too soon baby". "You would just be taking baggage into another relationship". "You need to heal sweetheart". "Get to know yourself better and find out what it is you are seeking". "Honey, it is way too soon for you to date right now". "Mom, it's too soon to even have dinner with someone"? "Pam, I read the Bible and love the Lord, love going to church, but sweetheart, don't get it twisted". "I bore you baby". "I know you better than you know yourself". "Spend some quality time with yourself baby". "It is okay to be alone; you don't always need a man in your life". "Mom, no Pam, it's not time to be with someone sweetheart". "Now I know you are going to do you, but I'm telling you baby you better listen to your mother on this one". "You see Pam, women think they can change men to be what they need and want them to be, no baby girl, it don't work like that". "You would be surprised to know that most good men love women who love themselves". "They can sense it when you don't feel good about yourself". "They take advantage of it and that is why you need a moment to yourself before you get back out there".

"Sweetheart the wounds you attain by exercising bravery will never make you feel inferior to the next man you come in contact with". "Once you get to know who you are, he won't sense insecurity from you". "A man like LB was broken when he met you, and if he didn't find himself before he found his wife, he was going to damage whomever he came in touch with down the line; prime example, you and his wife". "If there is someone out there interested in you, trust me, he will wait". "I really like Leon mom; what should I say to him". "You tell him that you spent the night with your mom and she said it is too soon to date"! "If he really cares about you Pam, he will wait". "Pam why would he want to date you and you just got out of a relationship"? "You should question that"! "Alright mom, I know you know best and would never tell me anything wrong". "That's right baby, how do you think I got your dad". "Girl you better go and ask somebody about me". "I don't know why I don't go and get a job counseling somewhere, oh, that's right, I counsel all six of my children, I don't have time for anyone else"! Lol! "Lady you are something else". "I know, and I love you and I want what's good for you baby". "I love you too mom and thanks for always being so honest with me". No problem, your bed is ready, go lie down now".

Chapter 23

Wow, I can't believe LB is still calling me. Five texts, really LB, haven't you had enough of texting? I should send them to his wife who seems to think that I'm breaking up happy homes. It's her husband who can't get enough of me. It's Friday and I want to be with Leon so bad. I know my mom warned me not to talk with him, but he seems so genuine. Mom is going to have to pray a little harder for me because I am going to call Mr. Leon.

"Hello Leon, hi Pam, how are baby"? "I hadn't heard from you I didn't know what to think; so I decided you probably needed some time". "Yes I did, I'm glad you didn't take offense to it". "No baby, I truly understand". "What's on your plate for tonight"? "I would like for you to be on my plate"! "Oh you got jokes"; "no baby I just couldn't resist that response, but I would like for you to be on my plate"! "Kevin Hart just came out with a new movie, and I heard it was hilarious". "He is funny, okay what time"? "Is four o'clock okay"? "That's cool". "You want me to come pick you up"? "No, Leon if it's okay I'll meet you at your place". "That's even better; maybe we can have a sip of wine before we head out". "Okay see you at about 4pm". "Hey Pam you want to do dinner before the movie or vice versa"? "Let's eat first and are we dressing casual"? "Yes, casual is cool". "Okay baby, I'll see you then". My mom is going to kill me! I can't help it. I like him and I love his hospitality. It feels so different to be somewhere else rather than staying at my house all the time; being at my house all the time made me feel so trapped. My mom is going to have to forgive me for this one but I'm doing me some Leon tonight. It was about 3ish and I headed on down to Leon's. All I could think about was how gentle this man was, and bam my phone started blowing up; you guessed it, LB. I thought to myself, brother you are not messing up my evening and hit reject! I continued on thinking if my mom knew that I had slept with Leon she would create me a new butt hole. Oh, but she won't know because I'm not telling her. I am going to deal with Leon like he's a married man. This has got to be on the low low!

I had on my most seductive jeans, my black top that shows my biceps and triceps, my favorite Michael Kors perfume on, hair down but off my face, make-up just right, and of course the 4 inch heels; OMG to myself! Yes, I must say I looked sassy tonight. I could not imagine what Leon was going to wear, but he would probably do something that would correlate with what I had on. Leon opened the door and I could have fallen into his arms. Like I said he had on some black jeans, a muscle shirt that was showing every muscle he owned, and a pair of Michael Kors penny loafers. Leon was 6'7," bald, his mustache and goatee connected; he was caramel complexion, with light brown eyes. He stayed in the gym, he had a physique you would not believe, in other words; very athletic. We both had a look on our faces that said let's not go to the movie. I walked in and he told me to make myself at home. I sat on his white leather sofa and he handed me a glass of wine. I felt so at home! We listened to a little jazz and sipped on our wine. I don't know why, but when I was with Leon I felt like we belonged together and it appeared that he felt the same way. As we got up to leave, he asked me if he could hug me and naturally I said yes. Well that hug led to a kiss. I broke away and said Leon this is only going to lead to some seductive activity that is going to keep us from our plans. "Okay Pam lets go baby". He locked up and we headed to SoHo's Steakhouse. We got into his triple black SUV Mercedes. Leon put some smooth jazz on and out of the blue asked me "Pam are you scared of me"? Where did that come from"? "Pam I really like you and I need you to know that I am not tripping off of the baggage between you and LB". Wow, funny that he used the same word that mom used. "I didn't think you were Leon". "I'm not scared of you, as a matter of fact, I feel quite comfortable with you". "Really, that's good to know". "You just made my evening baby; we can go as slow as you need to go". "You mean that Leon"? "Yes Pam I really mean that". "Let's get to know each other". I was happy on one hand, but sad on the other because I was hoping he didn't mean let's cut out the sex! OMG! I needed that part of the relationship. I know I just got out of that messy ass relationship with LB, but ya'll just don't know how Leon puts it down. Well, we will see what happens after tonight. If he doesn't try to seduce me, I won't press the issue. "Damn baby dinner was nice, but how about I fix us a night cap when we get back to my place"? "That sounds good". "What do you have a taste for Pam"? "I would love a strong cup of coffee". "Really"? "Yes really". "I know what Pam; my mom made a pound cake for dinner the other day and made me take some home". "How does pound cake and coffee sound"? "OMG! That sounds so good". "I am going to have to run an extra mile in the morning, but it will be well worth it".

"Me too, can I run with you in the morning"? "You sure can". "Do you run in the park or the gym Pam"? "Either or, but if I run the park I prefer running with someone". "I like it though whenever I do". "We can run the park, but I like to get out early Leon". "Well Ms. Pam we can get up together and go run". I'm thinking it is about to be on and popping now. "So Leon are you asking me to stay the night"? "You betta know it young lady, will you"? "Leon I thought we were taking it slow; we are baby, I just want to lie next to you and hold you all night". "Okay, that sounds good, but I need to get my gym bag out of the car". "Okay give me your keys and I'll get your bag out of your car. "Oh and baby can I go and take a shower while you are getting the coffee ready"? "Sure, the towels are in the closet". "OMG all I could think of was our first night together and look at my phone messages before he comes back in". "Leon was so good! As I stepped out of the shower; needless to say, he was back and had my towel in his hand and started drying me off". Well you know where that went. Every spot he dried off he would kiss me there. When he got to my legs he asked me to put them around his neck and he then started talking to Pam's Pearl. OMG! I finally mustered up enough energy to tell him let's have some coffee and cake. He complied. I didn't have any night clothes so Leon gave me one of his muscle t-shirts and we headed to the kitchen to finally have some coffee and cake. Leon had a look on his face that was so sincere. I thought to myself why couldn't I have met him first? Oh well, I didn't so moving right along….

Chapter 24

OMG! Is all I have to say is if I could wake up like this every morning; I would! This man was so incredibly gentle and yes we did go run and even the run was nice. He could barely keep up with me though! Lol! When Leon and I finished, I went home to shower and get my thoughts together. I called "D" to see what was going on with her and she was irritated as usual and it was probably Shaun who was irritating her. "What's up lady "D"? That fucken Shaun girl"! "I told you that you were going to either accept Shaun for who he was or leave him alone". "I keep telling you, you have nothing special that can change a man, didn't you read Steve Harvey's book"! "Yeah Pam, easy for you to say, you don't have to deal with him". "Let that man be who he is going to be and move on". "You chose to be in that situation thinking you were going to change him with what you had to offer".

"Shaun has been around the block and he will make a change when he wants to make the changes". "You can only change yourself and if you think that because you are all put together that's going to change him, it's not". "Anyone could see that Shaun is irresponsible to have all those kids and not married to one of the mother's". "Who does that"? "Now I'm not taking away his attributes, but come on "D," did you really think you were going to stop him from doing what he does"? That's what's wrong with women". "Some women think because they have it going on that men are going to change for them, no, they only change when they want to change". "The quicker we realize that the better off we'll be". "You are pretty, educated, no children and the first black female major on the police department". I mean really, and you want to settle for Shaun"? "I'm not trying to hurt your feelings, I just want you to know that you are better than that and deserve more".

"Pam, look how much time you spent with LB"? "D," this is not about me right now". "I have accepted my place with LB and I'm moving on". "D" why is it that every time I try to give you advice you try to play tit for tat with me about my life"? "Because you chose to deal with Shaun doesn't make you a loser". "I'm going to tell you what my mom told me, "disappointment is inevitable, but misery is a choice"! "You can't help how you feel". You need to learn to listen and deal with your self-esteem and stop comparing yourself to me". "I'm not your enemy"! "My bad Pam; I know you are trying to tell me what is right". "I just don't want to be looked upon as being stupid". "You are not the one that's stupid; it's that stupid motherfucker Shaun that's stupid". "You see "D" what we as women have to learn to do is love ourselves". "Men can tell when we are more into them than we are into ourselves". "If we spend the energy that we spend on them on us we would probably choose better men; and also when we choose we usually get nothing, when we wait on God and let the man choose us, we usually get the best". "When I'm talking to you "D" I'm talking to myself as well". "You should know by now that I am not one of those friends that tell you what you want to hear". "I'm either going to tell you how it is or I'm not going to tell you anything". "You have to deal from within in order to make a change for yourself". "The more you face yourself, the better you will start to feel good about yourself". "It is alright to be alone". "D" you got to stop thinking that you always need to be with someone; just stop and think..... . when was the last time you didn't have a man in your life"? "Ever since I have known you it has been one after the other". "That should be a clue to you". "Let me ask you something "D", are you scared to be alone"? "It appears that you don't want to face yourself, but that is the only way things are going to improve in your life".

My mom words echoed in my heart after telling talking "D". I know better than to be dealing with Leon. I know I should be searching my heart for some answers about me. I can't blame LB for the eleven years I spent with him. I knew damn well what I was doing and he never made me continue on in the relationship. Those were choices I made and must deal with. "D" you the only reason that I got with Leon was so I didn't have to think about what was going on in my life. That ugly truth is what my mom called it. She always told me that most time we think we are in control. We don't realize that we maintain control when we give up trying to control people. Oh no, we look at it as being weak. That is why we suffer so much. "D" it's like you on your job as a leader; a leader has to create space so that others can feel they are a part of the team, otherwise, your team will just exist". "When you are exemplifying leadership, you want to show them that you also know how to be under authority". "You should have compassion for

people but at the same time you don't want to
compromise principle, and most importantly you
should be approachable, meaning you should lead
by understanding and not intimidate people". "You
are watching how the men on this department are
operating and you know you didn't like what you
went through". "Remember T. D. Jakes sermon
that we saw on TV when he said "It is not the
destination that solidifies you; it is the things you
learned along the way". "Pam you remember that"?
"Oh yes ma'am and I keep those words close to my
heart". "I don't want to make other people
accountable for my actions; I must take
accountability for my own actions before any type
of improvement can take place in my life". "D"
most of the times you are not mad at me nor
Shaun". "You just don't want to be accountable for
your own stuff". "You don't want to own your
stuff because it causes you to face yourself and
you're scared to see who you really are"! "D" until
you are ready to see yourself for who you really are,

your life is not going to change"! Pam I want you to know that I really do love our talks in spite of me always playing the tit for tat game"!

Chapter 25

It's a beautiful morning!   Oh how I love that song.
It was a beautiful until I got that call from Leon. I
could not believe what I was hearing. He told me
that they walked "D" out of the precinct today. I
could not believe the reason! Laundering drug
money! She told me she stopped! Leon could not
get into the whole story because he was at work,
but he told me he would call me later and give me
the 411. I wanted to call LB because I knew he
knew the scoop. "What's up LB"? "Hi baby, how
are you doing these days"? "I'm fine". "LB you
know why I called you, I know you know the word
is out". "What happened to my girl"? "Pam, the
word is that she was set up". "Set up how"?
"Somebody came in on her". "They set up cameras
on the last bust they made and they have her on
camera putting the money in a bag and walking out
of the precinct and to her car with it". "Wow"! "I

told her ass to stop that shit". "She makes enough money on her own; she did not have to steal". "I know Pam, but once you start doing it, getting away with it, it's hard to stop". "You start thinking you are above the law". "Oh, is that how it was for you"? "Pam where are you going with this"? "You know damn well where I'm going with this". "Is that how you were able to take care of me the way you did"? "Is that where the down payment for my house came from"? "No Pam, I took care of you the way I did because I love you baby and I still do". "Whatever LB"! "So what's her next step LB"? "Well they are going back and investigating all of the drug busts she was in charge of". "Then what's next"? "Pam to be honest with you baby, the way Pam did MR, she has no chance". "What"? "He is out to get her"! OMG! "Pam have you talked to her yet"? "No, I wanted to find out what was going on because I know when I do she is going to ask me to call you". "Pam can I come by the house and tell you what is really going on"?

"Yes LB, what time can you get here"? "I'm on my way baby". Damn I should not have told him he could come here. I like me some Leon, but I really did love LB and to be quite honest with you, I think I still do. Ring..... ."Damn did you fly over"? "Oh, you a comedian now". "No, I'm just saying, you made it here quick". "How are you baby"? "I'm fine LB, what's going on"? "Pam can I just hold you for a minute, baby I miss you so much". Hugging............ why am I letting this man hug me. I know what his touch does to me. "Okay LB, let me go". "Baby let me have you; I need and miss you so much". When LB started kissing me I knew what this was going to lead to. I tried so hard to resist, but I must admit, even though I liked me some Leon, LB was good and when I felt that woody, then he went to the pearl... You guessed it! I submitted to LB and it was just as I remembered. OMG! I could not believe that I fell in this trap again. I actually missed him. He was so good that I forgot he came over to tell me about

"D". "LB we need to talk about "D's" situation". "I know baby, let me gather myself, Pam I missed you so much and I can tell you missed me as well". "LB, this is not about you and me right now". "What is going on with my girl"? "Pam you know how MR is and "D" thinks she can just do as she pleases; but you know that's not how this game is played". "MR is out for "D's" throat". "He said he was humiliated and no woman was going to neither humiliate him nor get away with humiliating him on his job; he made her what she was"! "He said that will never happen". "You know she was still messing with Shaun and he despises him". "I don't know why, they are just alike". "He just had more power than Shaun". "He was just mad because Shaun wasn't scared of his ass". "Well all the same baby, she is gone". "She will be lucky if she don't get jail time". "What"! "Are you serious LB"? "As a heart attack Pam". "So what do you suggest I tell her"? "I think she should resign and disappear"! "OMG"! "Disappear like how"? "Leave the department"? "Yes ma'am"! "She is going to go out of her mind". "Pam, "D" has a degree now; she could go to the board of education and teach until she gets herself together". "I know she got paper saved up". "If she resigns, she will leave with at least 100,000. 00 with her rank and the drop program". "I know "D" saved some of that money". "LB you know how she likes to live". "You see the car she drives". "Damn, this is her calling now". "I'm going to reject it for a minute; I got to get my thoughts together". "Is this her texting me now"? Oh shit that's Leon! (Leon) "What's up baby" (text)? Damn! Let me text him back. "Hi baby, I will call you when I get freed up, I'm talking to "D". No response.... that's strange. I bet he sees LB's car in front of the house. Fuck! "Was that Pam baby"? "Yes, I told her I would call her back when you leave". "Pam I love and miss you so much". "LB, I can't do the lies baby". "Pam after all that my wife did, she knows I love you". "She refuses to divorce me". "She says that there is no way that she is giving up all that she helped me build". "Pam she even put me out of the bedroom". "She said the house is big enough for us to live in and not get in each other's' way". "Pam I am miserable"! "LB, I can't live this way baby". "I miss you but I want my own man". "Baby you do have me to yourself". "Don't you see what she is doing"? "I went to my lawyer and he advised me to just sit it out and hopefully she will want to divorce me eventually". "Baby please don't throw us away"! "LB we'll talk, right now I need to talk to "D". "Are you asking me to leave baby"? "Yeah baby, but not like that LB, I just don't want to talk about us right now". "Okay Pam, I understand. I need to get back to the precinct anyway, but I will call you shortly". "Okay, I might have to text you because "D" might have some questions that you can answer". "Okay, do you mind if I take a shower before I go"? "It's cool, let me know when you leave; I'm going to go in the den and call her". "Okay". OMG, what did I just do? I can't believe I just made love to that man like we never stopped. I can't believe my girl is getting ready to get canned or maybe even go to jail! What the fuck is going on? Maybe I'll start with some positive shit first. Hell naw, "D" is going to want to hear the truth. Let me call her while LB is taking a shower. "Hey "D" what's up"? "Girl you talk to LB"? "I know you heard I got walked out yesterday". "I tried to call you but it just went to voicemail". "Yeah girl I heard". "LB is over here now". "What"! "Yeah, girl, I'll explain it later". "OMG"! "Pam tell me you didn't give him none"? "Okay I won't tell you". "But I did, however, we don't need to be discussing me right now". "I thought you told me you quit stealing drug money "D"? "Pam the last drug bust was so easy I said to myself that that was going to be the last one I took from". "D," girl you didn't need any money, why"? "You make 120,000. 00 a year"! "What are you thinking"? "Are you gambling"? "I know you're not doing drugs because you love your body".

"Pam I'm gambling". "What"? "What is wrong with you "D"? "Pam please don't judge me". "Please don't judge me". "D" you are tripping girl". "Just tell me what LB said". "D" you need to just resign". "Fuck No"! "I'm not going down without a fight"! "D," you are on camera baby". "What are you going to fight"? "LB said you might even get jail time". "What"! "Yes jail time"! "OMG"! "Pam what is going on with me"? "D," LB suggest that you resign and just go on and apply at the board of education and teach for a minute until you collect yourself or maybe even go to one of the municipalities if you want to continue in police business. "No Pam, if I resign from this shit, I'm done"! "D" every successful person has found a way to face and overcome the hurdles they run into that tries to destroy some of their vision in their lives". "You are intelligent, educated, and still young". "You have time to start a new career girl". "You can go back and get your masters' degree". "Pam a degree don't mean shit". "I know lots of people with degrees and don't know more than me". "Maybe not, but on paper they know more than yo ass"!. "Go apply for a job and don't have a degree and the other person has one, I guarantee you they will look at the other applicant before they look at you; and if they look at you it's because they are going to pay you less! "D" you remember the big controversy when Steve and John were up for the major's position and they wanted Steve, but John had his BA degree so they had to give it to John"? "It makes a difference when you finish talking all that crazy talk". "You might as well go back and get your masters". "You don't have that much to finish so why are you debating about it"? Pam whatever!   Okay whatever; you just better go back so you can start you a new career off strong; your BA is cool, but your Masters is going to get you in somebodies door quicker". "Leaving the police department is not the end of the world; people do it every day". "I know Pam; I think it's the way I'm leaving that bothers me". "I feel like this motherfucker MR won". "No "D," it's not about him right now, it's about you and you need to resign, not go to jail". "People leave for worse reason's than this". "About this gambling "D," how did you get caught up in that"? "Pam I had so much money that I didn't know what to do with it". I shop whenever I get ready, how many clothes can one person have"? I got the finest ride, hell I got bored one day, couldn't find any of my boy toys, so I went to the casino". "I had the nerve to be enjoying the shit". "It was like a get a way for me". "Almost like working out". "However, the rest is history; I like going on the boat"!

Chapter 26

"D" and I must have talked for hours. She finally understood where I was coming from and what we planned out for her was the best thing for her to do at this time. "D" had a birthday coming up and after we talked about her resigning we started talking about what we were going to do for her birthday. Even though she was not in that type of mood, we came up with a girls wine sip. "D's" home was the perfect spot. She had an in ground swimming pool where the upper deck overlooked it and a hot tub that seats 10 people. Her place was to die for! "We made the plans and put together a list of people who we could stomach. I finally looked at my phone and saw all of the messages and texts I missed and told her I would catch up to her later. Now I'm trying to figure out how I am going to tell Leon that I cannot see him anymore. Damn, my mom told me not to fuck with him! I am so sorry, but my heart is with LB. He'll get over it. Ring....... (Calling Leon) "Hey Pam, I was hoping you would see my text and call me". "Hi Leon; we need to talk". "Is everything okay Pam". "Yeah, everything is cool, just need to holler at you about some things". "I can't see you anymore". "Why Pam"? "I should have never started seeing you and I hadn't cleaned up my baggage with LB". "Pam, what are you saying baby"? "I'm saying that I spent 11 years with that man, and whether I was going to stop seeing him or not, I still shouldn't have started seeing you". "I wasn't ready for a relationship Leon; I just didn't want to be alone". "I'm so sorry if I caused you any pain, confusion, or discomfort". "Okay baby". "I hope we can continue to be cordial". "Okay Pam". Damn, did I just leave that fine ass nigga alone and he was alright with it? Shit there was no way that the two of them was going to deal with me and know it. "D's" crazy ass would have figured out how to make that shit work! Oh well, I couldn't do it. Now let me call LB's ass back so I see how we are going to do this shit. I am not going to be so kind if Mrs. Brown approach me again. I am going to put her in her place and she is going to have to do what she gotta do. Ring......(Calling LB) "Hi baby, hey LB". "What did "D" decide on doing"? "She's going to resign". "Good for her baby, because it was not looking good for her". "LB what makes MR think he can do people like that"? "Baby, when you got that much power, you can do whatever you want to do". "LB that's not right". "That man is married, she didn't owe him exclusivity". "His ass is going to pay"! "Baby, can I come back over this evening"? "Yes LB, because we need to talk". "I know sweetheart". "Let me get some things squared away and I'll be through". "Okay". I wonder why "D" is texting me? OMG! "Pam; come over right away"! I'm thinking what in the hell is wrong with "D"! I called LB and told him that I am going over to "D's" house and I would call him when I am headed back home. I walked in and "D" was hysterically crying. I finally calmed her down and I could not believe that MR called her and said the chief wanted to know if she was going to resign or take a board trial. This bastard had some kind of nerve. "D" what did you say to him"? "I told him I was resigning". "What did MR say"? "He just said good luck and advised me where to bring all of my department gear so that I could sign my resignation papers and receive my last check and my 401K monies". "Wow, and he was the one who had to make that call"? "Unbelievable"! "Yeah Pam, he did that". "I am so upset; I really don't want to have the wine sip". "I understand, "D," but you got to keep on moving girlfriend". "You can't let him see you sweat". "As hard as it may seem, you got to go on with life as if nothing has ever happened". "The best revenge is success"! "Did you tell Shaun what happened"? "No not yet; I really don't want to talk to his broke ass right now". "D" we are going to go ahead and have our wine sip and celebrate you girl". "The police department is not going to break you". "As a matter of fact, have you applied for a subbing position with the board of education yet"? "Yep, and guess what "D," since I was the police major, they want me to work in their alternative school as the dean of students; girl I get benefits as well". "That's what I'm talking about, but "D" you still need to go back and get your Master's Degree". "Okay Pam, how many times are you going to say that"? "As many times as it takes"! How do you feel "D"? Girl I am hurting. "Girl I can't believe this motherfucker would do this to me". "Well believe it; LB said he can be overbearing at times". "Well so can I; you can best believe he is going to get his baby". "I mean that, you can take that to the bank"! "So what's up with you and Leon"? "Girl, I can't do him". I'm so deeply in love with LB". "Pam, are you serious". "You are going to still do him"? "Yes I am "D"". "But Pam, what about his wife"? "What about her"? "I'm meeting LB in a minute and we are going to have a long talk about this mess". "D," I know he loves me and it's not like an affair, like a lot of these brothers are out here doing". "This man does everything with me in public, with my family, and he takes care of me financially". "D" he spends the night like he lives there". He actually has his own closet and chest space". "Ever since I moved out of the Brooks house, he has just been magnificent with helping me". "He pays my house note, buys groceries and he brought Tyrone his first car". "I love him "D". "He has been more of a dad to Tyrone than his own dad". "Pam you sure you're not with him because you think you owe him"? "Girl I left the best part out, my sexual life is what most women only dream about"! "Girl so what are you going to do about Leon". "D" let me tell you something my mom told me during one of our sessions: Why would Leon knowingly want to date me and realize that I just got out of an eleven year relationship with LB"? "What is that about"? "Pam he probably wanted to make LB think he could take his woman that he had for eleven years". "Girl he couldn't possibly think that, word in the precincts is that he can't keep a woman because he is so into himself". "He probably fucks himself; he thinks he is that fine". "But, "D" lets' give the brother his props', he is fine as that thang, got a hell of a body and good in bed"! "Well I can't speak on that last thing you put out there, but the other two, show you right"! "Hey "D," you know after a little pillow talk with Leon he told me that you tried to holler at him and when he didn't want to holler back you gave him hell". "What was up with that"? "Girl, that nigga lying"! "He just didn't like working for women so we kept clashing". "D" you can tell me the truth, he wasn't the only one I heard that from". "He's fine and I can understand you wanting to get with him, but you got to know that just because you look nice doesn't mean that everyone is going to want you"! "You know your attitude leaves a lot to be desired sometimes; after a while, all of that cuteness turns sour"! LMAO!

"Whatever Pam"! "It's all good girl, I'm done with him, you can go after him now"! "Really, thanks but no thanks"! "Alright, I'm glad you feel better, I getting ready to meet LB". "Pam you need to leave that man alone". "Yeah, and you need to go back to school and leave Shaun alone". "We can do this all night baby"! "Ok go ahead and do you; I will make sure I'm there when she asks to meet with your ass again". "Ok Ms. "D" you go jokes, I will holler at you tomorrow". "See Ya"!

Chapter 27

OMG! This has been a long day. I really don't want to talk to LB. I am exhausted; all I want to do is take a bubble bath and have a glass of wine. I need to think about this relationship with him. I know my mom is going to strangle me if I tell her I'm even considering dealing with LB again. Sometimes I think that people should have a little more understanding for those who just can't help themselves. I know I need to tell myself what I tell others; excuses are for incompetent people. Hell, that's how I feel right about now. It has been an unbelievable month! First me meeting with LB's wife and now my girl "D" is quitting the police department. Man I wished she had listened to me. She was always debating with me every time I tried to fore warn her about things. I knew it was because I had my Master's Degree; she felt I thought I knew everything. That really wasn't the case. I was getting my information from LB and I thought she would appreciate that. But every time I tried to inform her she would say Shaun said this and that. Well you see where she landed. Where is Shaun now? Probably telling her not to resign, but if she know what's good for her she better resign. With all of the babies that nigga had, how she could believe anything he had to say was beyond my state of comprehension. It was apparent that he was irresponsible but for whatever reason; "D" loved her some Shaun and Shaun loved him some women. With "D" leaving the department, I know Shaun is going to have a field day with the other female officers. Most of them were glad to see her ass gone. They hated her because she was smart, cute, and took care of her body. Well, no that wasn't really why they hated her; they hated her because of her nasty disposition. "D" walked around like she was the Chief of Police. The men loved her and she loved them. She could talk her way out of anything. Anything but the shit she's in now. I need to call her and see when she's taking her police gear in and getting what they owe her monetarily.

"Hey "D," what up"? "Hey Pam, I'm just chilling girl". "I am so not looking forward to taking this shit downtown". "Girl you need to go ahead and get it over with". "You want me to go with you"? "No, I'm good". "Thanks though". "I'll hit you when I get back". "Okay "D," it's going to be all good". I knew "D" had the strength to go downtown by herself, but I also knew she had that fight in her and she wanted to give MR a run for his money. Not a wise decision! She had it going on and all she needed to do was find herself another
` somewhere else to go. Believe me when she starts at the BOE it is going to be on again. "D" is going to give those people the blues. She is going to step in there like she has already been there. I heard most educators in that type of setting don't like to be told anything because of their education. I can

see some issues before she gets started. I am just hoping that "D" goes back to school and finish her education.

Chapter 28

"What's up Pam, hey "D" how did it go"? "Girl have you talked to LB"? "No, why"? "Girl I got something for that MR"! "Girl what happened"? "Did you drop off everything"? "Yes and when I got there who you think happened to be in the office watching me sign for my shit"? "You guessed it; that punk ass motherfucker". "Well "D" it's over now girl". "No Pam, it's not over until I say it's over". "I'm not through with his ass". "D" let that shit go and move on girl". "Don't let him consume you with anger". "Trust me that motherfucker is missing your ass". "I tell you what "D," the best way to get his ass is to be successful". "Go back to school and finish your masters' degree". "Do what you need to do to move forward". "As long as you sit back and plot on him you are only going to prolong your destiny". "You know what I always say "Don't give him power over you". "Girl I can't stand his ass". "I just can't believe how all that shit went down "D". "Have you talked to LB"? "No, not today". "I'm not looking forward to talking to him". "Why"? "D" this motherfucker wants to live life like he's the Golden King". "I love him, but I know this shit ain't right". "My mom is so disappointed that I even got mixed up with him". "What and how she feels means so much to me". "Pam that shit you are pondering over should be a no brainer; and that shit you are pondering over should be a no brainer as well". "I know, but Pam that shit shouldn't have went down like that". "D" just be glad your ass didn't go to jail and count your blessings girl". I can't believe she feels like somebody is doing her wrong and she was the one stealing money! Wow! "Pam if you could have seen him watching me sign those resignation papers with that shit eatin grin on his face". "I could have snapped his fucken neck". "D" you got a good job with BOE, which most folks couldn't have even gotten with the way you left, I mean really"? "Let that shit go and start over". "You always giving out advice, are you taking your own damn advice"? "Apparently not, you are still pondering over LB ass"! "Girl go sit down somewhere". "My pondering has nothing to do with LB at this time; I am tripping off of my parents because I let this motherfucker back into my life". "I love him but the fact that he thinks he can live life like the Golden King". "D" this is my mom let me hit you back". "Okay later".

OMG! "D" is going to drive herself nuts! I mean really, how in the hell can she think she has a fight with the PD with all of the evidence they have on her? This girl really thinks her shit don't stink! I can't wait for her to start her new job with the BOE; just maybe her life may take a turn for the better. Damn, who is this calling me? "What's up LB"? "Hi baby, you sound a little frustrated". "Not really, just got through dealing with "D's" ass". "What's up with her"? "LB she is still talking about suing the PD and getting back at MR". "Well if she know like I do baby she would leave well enough alone". "LB she is serious, I think she has something on him". "Really, well it better be good because he has as much power as the chief". "You know one day I was talking to her and she kind of slip and said something about a video and I didn't press the issue because "D" is always doing something with her little boy toys so I never said anything". "So what are you thinking she has baby"? "LB, I would be willing to bet that she has a video of them having sex"! OMG! "Baby no"! "Yep, she sounded to secure about it". "But baby that doesn't negate the fact that they have her on camera stealing money". "I know, but I just believe that girl is up to something". "LB you don't know "D". "D" moves smooth when it comes to protecting herself and messing with men that she knows has more power than her". "Yeah baby I hear you, but you don't know MR". "Girl I have seen some shit in my twenty plus years with motherfuckers that has crossed him". "Well time is going to tell". "I think she is keeping something from me and because of my dealings with you; she thinks I will tell you and you will arm MR". "That's possible; well only time will tell".

"So baby can we go out and talk about getting our relationship back on track"? "LB we have a lot of talking to do". "I am very skeptical about getting a one on one relationship with you". "Pam, you know how I feel and I know you love me". "Okay, and what"? "Baby don't do this to us; I told you what was going on with my wife and how she was doing things". "Yeah, I know that's what you say LB". "Let me tell you this darling; your wife can't come to me anymore"! "She got a break the first time, the next time I'm giving it to her"! I understand Pam and I promise you that won't happen anymore baby". "I still have some pondering to do baby". "What Pam"? "LB if something happens to you where does this leave me"? "Your wife gets everything". "I will be left here crying without a pot to piss in". "I can't grow old with you and plan retirement". "I mean how long do you think we can do this"? "Pam baby I will take out a policy and put it you and your son's name". "Baby I mean business about you". "I love you Pam and if my wife wasn't acting like she is, I would divorce her and marry you baby". "Really"! "Yes Pam I would". "I love you and Tyrone". "So how do I explain this to my family"? "You do know my mom knows about you"? "Pam I am so serious about you and Tyrone, that I will talk to your mom myself". "Damn baby you are serious huh"? "Yes Pam, I am serious". Baby can we go out to dinner tonight"? "Yeah, I'll call you and let you what time I'll be ready to leave". "Okay baby I'll see you then".

Chapter 29

How am I going to deal with my family**???** I know this is not what I should be doing, but I really love LB. I really believe he's not dealing with his wife emotionally or physically. Both of them have checked out on one another and are just going through technicalities. My parents are not going for this and I know it. I guess it's time for my overnight mom talk. Damn what does "D" want? "What's up "D"? "Girl, have you heard"? "Heard what"? "You still haven't talked with LB"? "Yeah I did". "He didn't tell you"? "Tell me what "D"? "Stop playing and just tell me girl". "Pam that motherfucker MR got what he deserved". "What "D"? "He is downtown turning in his shit". "I only wished that I could have been there to see his face". "Girl I heard somebody turned in a video with that motherfuckers' ass in the air"! "What"! "D" you got tell me what you are talking about girl". "Are you home"? "I'm on my way over "D," keep talking girl". "When did this come out"? "Girl I heard an anonymous video was sent to IAD and MR was called in to view it and the rest is history". "D" where do you suppose it came from"? "Girl I don't know, don't care, just glad it happened". "I'm outside, open the door". "D" what do you mean a video, did they say what was on it". "Well you know it have to be something provocative if that motherfucker resigned". "D" did you have something to do with that"? "Now Pam, why is it that every time something scandalous happens; you place me at the scene of the crime"? "Because I know you can be scandalous". "Oh well"! "Wow this is LB calling me".

"I bet it's about MR". "What's up baby"? "Baby you got a minute, yeah what's up"? "I can't do dinner tonight because I need to meet with MR". "What happened"? " I don't know but he sounded very upset". "Can I come by when I finish"? "Sure, I'll see you then".

"Girl something did go down with MR". "Good for his ass"! "Did LB go into details"? "No he didn't, he said he would get with me later because he had to go meet MR". "D" I know your ass had something to do with this". "Whatever Pam"! "Well I'm going to go over to moms and see what's cooking over there". "Pam, are you going to tell her about you and LB". "Nope"! "Why not"? "That conversation will have to be one of our overnighters; you know how we do it". "I want to know what happened to MR". "You are a bit too calm for me "D"; "I know your hands are in this some kind of way". "Pam, MR is getting what he deserves, I don't know how it happened, I'm just glad it happened to his ass"! "How about that"! "I am taking your advice and I am focusing on starting my new job with the MBOE on Monday".

Coming soon.......

"How was your first week "D"? "Girl you know I went in there clean as the board of health". "I felt daggers all around me". "Bitches were whispering like the niggas did when we started the police department". "Pam, most of these bitches look tired as hell". "Girl they are all out of shape, dress attire is something awful". OMG! "And they are professionals", really? "The men; girl they look so pitiful, it was unreal; nothing like the PD". "The one's with their PhD's has got their heads so far up their ass it is unreal". "It appears that their education means more than those children they serve". "Girl so much for that, what went down with MR"? "Girl "D" this motherfucker videotaped some prostitute giving him some head, among other things". "You got to be kidding me"? "What is wrong with him"! "His career and marriage is over". "What in the hell did he get out of videotaping that bullshit"? "Hell, the motherfucker barely turned on the lights when we were together". "What could his fat ass possibly want to see"? "No "D," the question is how did the tape get out"? "I don't know Pam". "Okay "D," I told you that all you had to do was sit back and wait; people's behavior good, bad, or indifferent, will always uncover, and sure enough he uncovered himself". "I want all the details Pam; you need to call me when you finish talking to LB". "It has got to be more to this story". "You are probably right". "Anyway, how was your first week"?

"Girl you would not believe how these educated people act". "What do you mean "D"? "I was sitting in the main office waiting for the principal when I heard one of the secretaries Chell, the one that flunked out of the police academy, yeah I didn't know she came to work for the board of education; "Yes I remember her; I talk with her periodically and I knew she worked for the BOE". "While I was waiting on the principal I heard her on the phone". "It sounded like she was trying to advise a parent about an embarrassing situation regarding her child and somehow the conversation got off track and went sour". "The parent must have called back and asked for the principal and after their conversation she was called into the principal's office".

"Pam, I swear to you I can't make this shit up, the conversation went like this: "Ms. Fairly can I see you in my office please". "Yes ma'am". "Ms. Fairly you have been in my office three times now and I'm going to need you to get it together". "Now Pam, at this point I expected the principal to close her door, but she didn't". "She continues to tell Chell that she had three complaints regarding the way she had been answering the phone". "She started to rant and rave about her leaving people on hold much too long and talking down to people; and then asked her to explain it to her". "Girl I was embarrassed for Chell". "But anyhow she said: "well Dr. Jones, a student came into the office and asked to use the phone". "I was ear hustling and when she got off the phone she said in a low tone, "all of those kids are going to laugh at me". "I asked her why; she said she soiled her clothes and you can see blood on her pants". "I asked her if she would like for me to call her mom; She said yes". Pam, Chell looked so embarrassed; she continued to tell the principal that she didn't realize that the young lady had been to the nurse and the nurse had already called her mom". "Chell was so concerned about the child that she said she called the child's mom from the school phone and when the parent didn't answer, she called her mom from her personal phone and she answered". Really! She advised Dr. Jones that she told the child's parent who she was and why she was calling her". She then told Dr. Shantay Jones what the parent said; "Ma'am I guess she thinks because you called that something would change; I told the nurse that I didn't have transportation and this is not my problem". Chell told the parent that it was her problem and ours as well, that's why I'm calling you". "Oh! You gettin smart with me," "no ma'am, I'm not being smart. I'm saying to you that your daughter is right, if she goes to class with blood on her, the kids will laugh at her and she would be humiliated and devastated". Pam, she told Dr. Jones that the parent asked to speak to the principal and at that time she transferred the call. Girl Dr. Jones said "Well Ms. Fairly you are going to have to be a little bit softer to our customers". So I guess Chell must have gotten tired of Dr. Jones tone and said "You know Dr. Jones, I understand you and everything, but I think that's what is wrong with this system now". "We don't hold our parents accountable for anything and the minute one goes downtown because they don't like hearing the truth, we get scared and want to chastise personnel about it". "Parents don't want to hear the truth but as long as we are giving them something, the system is alright, the minute we call them on the carpet, they threaten us and say they are going to call the superintendent". "Well Ms. Fairly there is nothing I can do about that, but when I get calls from downtown, I have to address it". "On another matter Ms. Fairly, the staff is saying that you are not helping out the way Ms. Friends did and I am getting complaints that you are putting staff on hold for much too long as well". "Dr. Jones let's get something straight right now; first of all I am not Ms. Friends. Secondly, I am not the teacher's personal secretary". "When I introduced myself to you and told you why I thought I was placed at your school you told me that this was a family environment and we will make it work here". "Since that time I have been in your office three times and the atmosphere is far from being like a family". "You have yet to give me directions on how things should be done, you just call me in when there is a complaint and as a result I do things the way I know how". "You then tell me that other staff members are complaining about me because I asked them if they could ask someone else to help them out because I was busy answering the phone". "You even said that the phones can be overwhelming because we get an influx of calls daily". "With that being said, why did we even have to have this conversation"? "That's like telling a person that's an alcoholic that I know you are an alcoholic, but here have a drink". "Dr. Jones if you know that the phones are busy and you know I'm new to your building, you would think that you would have them to work with me". "I am tired of hearing that Ms. Friends did this and that". "I am not Ms. Friends"! "How about can you tell your counselor's and your other secretary to let me know if they are out to lunch or in a meeting"!

"Out of respect they could at least call me and let me know they are not available". "Well Ms. Fairley you should call them first and see if they are busy with someone before you send the call to them". "Excuse me, are you serious"? "You just said that we get a lot of calls and you want me to call everyone first to see if they are busy before I put a call through"? "Really"? "I don't think so Dr. Jones". "People would never get through if I did that". "I can't believe you would even suggest something like that". "I'll tell you what Dr. Shantay Jones, I think I need my union rep to finish this conversation". "Can we meet on next Thursday"? "We certainly can Ms. Fairly".

Ring, Ring, Ring, Hello? "Mr. Race this is Ms. Fairly". "I am scheduled to have a meeting with my principal on next Thursday, can you be there"? "Yes ma'am". "As a matter of fact we will talk on Wednesday, the day before so that we can prep". "Ok, thanks, I appreciate that". "How is everything else going Ms. Fairly"? "I'm good, but I will fill you in on Wednesday; okay, talk to you then".

Ring, Ring, Ring…Hello? What's up Pam? Nothing, what's going on Chell? "I heard you were over at the school "D" is working in".

"Yes girl and ever since I transferred over here I have caught nothing but hell"! "Pam these motherfuckers' over here are crazy". "I sit here and I'm thinking, these people are educated, I can't believe it sometimes". "If they are not acting like idiots, they are dressing like idiots". "Pam these motherfuckers' go out to lunch and won't even say "hey Ms. Fairly, I won't be available for an hour, can you hold my calls"? "They hold meetings, go to lunch, and anything else before telling me anything". "I have never seen anything like it". "It's nothing like the clerks that answer the phone at the PD". "We are talking highly educated people, Really? "Then the fucken principal thinks her shit don't stink and she looks just like her ghetto ass name "Dr. Shantay Jones"! "She thinks this shit is cool, I think she abuses her power". "From the kids to the adults, I don't know which is worse". "If people would only realize that when you share your power it doesn't take anything from you, it just empowers everyone"! "Any hoo, girl I called to tell you that "D" is working over here in the attendance department". OMG! "The one thing I can say is that "D" is going to give them a run for their money". "She was in the office waiting on Dr. Shantay Jones and heard all of what was going on"; "yeah Chell she told me girl". "Imagine her impression on her first day; really"? "D" told me she thought that she recognized you, and that they was on some doo-doo over there". "But you know "D" ain't having it"! "It is about to go DOWN AT MSLSD"!